THE MOST SINGULAR ADV  **)N**

Other books by Eleanor Berry

Tell us a Sick One Jakey
Never Alone with Rex Malone
The Ruin of Jessie Cavendish
Your Father Died on the Gallows
Robert Maxwell as I Knew Him
Seamus O'Rafferty and Dr Blenkinsop
Alandra Varinia Seed of Sarah
The House of the Mad Doctors
Jaxton the Silver Boy
Someone's Been Done up Harley
O, Hitman, my Hitman!
McArandy was hanged under Tyburn Tree
The Scourging of Poor Little Maggie
The Revenge of Miss Rhoda Buckleshott

Some comments.

Never Alone with Rex Malone
   ("A ribald, ambitious black comedy, a story powerfully told"). *The Daily Mail*

   ("I was absolutely flabbergasted when I read it!") *Robert Maxwell*

Your Father Died on the Gallows
   ("A unique display of black humour which somehow fails to depress the reader.") Craig McLittle. *The Rugby Gazette*

Robert Maxwell as I Knew Him
   ("One of the most amusing books I have read for a long time. Eleanor Berry is an original.") Elisa Seagrave. *The Literary Review*
   ("Undoubtedly the most amusing book I have read all year.") Julia Llewellyn Smith. *The Times*

The Scourging of Poor Little Maggie
   "This harrowing, tragic and deeply ennobling book, caused me to weep for two days after reading it. I had not experienced this reaction since seeing the film *The Elephant Man*.") Moira McClusky. *The Cork Evening News*.

THE MOST SINGULAR ADVENTURES OF EDDY VERNON

Eleanor Berry

ARTHUR H. STOCKWELL LTD.
Elms Court   Ilfracombe   Devon
Established 1898

All characters and situations portrayed in this book are imaginary. Any resemblance to persons living or dead is purely coincidental.

©Eleanor Berry 1998.
First published in Great Britain, 1998.

British Library Cataloguing in Publication Data.
A catalogue record for this book is available from the British Library.

ISBN 0 7223 3232-7

Printed in England by Arthur H. Stockwell Ltd., Ilfracombe, Devon.

Cover design by Eleanor Berry, Eddy Taylor and Harry Hobbs.

Cover printed in England by Arthur H. Stockwell Ltd., Ilfracombe, Devon.

For my good friend, William Hurndell, who has taken, and continues to take, a lively, animated and passionate interest in my writings.

E.B.

On a wet afternoon in early September 1995, a huge number of mourners attended a Norman church in the East End of London. There was an extensive area of graves surrounding it, making it look tiny and ant-like, and nearly invisible from the outer part of the cemetery.

The first mourner to arrive was a man called Eddy Vernon. The ceremony was not due to take place until 2.00 p.m., but he was already there at 12.30, and made a point of sitting closest to the aisle.

Vernon was in his fifties. His head, which had once been bald to avoid recognition, was covered with short, thick, greyish black hair.

He was not overtly handsome, but his appearance was not unattractive. His features were distinctive and even, and his eyes large, brown and bloodshot. They carried an air of fragility, which suggested that their owner had suffered from stress and abuse during his childhood, and most of his adult life. His skin was yellow and he looked unwell.

He leant forward, knowing he was alone and took a bottle of whisky from his briefcase. He took a few swigs with a sense of urgency, before putting the bottle away.

The funeral due to take place was that of Vernon's mother, Olive. He was the youngest of three sons. Kelvin was the oldest. He bore a strong facial resemblance to Eddy. The next son's name was Alan, who was three years Kelvin's junior, and blonde. Eddy was five years younger than Alan.

In the mid 1950s, the Vernons had lived in a rough area in London's East End, near Bethnal Green. The head of the family, Olive's husband, Ernest Vernon, had died fifteen years before his widow, and had been too ill with heart disease for most of his adult years, to qualify as the family breadwinner.

Olive Vernon, the formidable family matriarch, died of cancer in 1995. Before then, she had enjoyed rude and faultless health. Long before illness struck her down at the age of fifty, she was as tough and resilient as a vitamin-laden thirty-five year old.

Unemployment was high in the East End in the fifties and honest work was hard to come by. Olive and her three sons lived and mixed in the criminal fraternity, the only *modus vivendi* available to them.

They lived through crime in the East End, and sometimes in the West End, where they blackmailed extortionist landlords, exploiting educationally subnormal immigrants. They operated at least a decade before the Kray brothers of later years occupied the limelight in that milieu.

The Vernons kept a lower profile than the

Krays, but were respected by those they were kind to, and feared by anyone who crossed them, which made them almost immune to arrest.

They dealt in hard drugs, protection rackets and other enterprises, considered by the Law to be "naughty". The three brothers also served as hitmen to anyone rich enough to pay them to commit murder.

They were not exclusively wicked, however. They were chivalrous and protective towards elderly people, women and children. These vulnerable parties felt safer than before to walk through London streets at night, carrying valuables with them, under the umbrella of the protective Vernons, whom many of them looked upon as heroes.

Kelvin and Alan, Eddy's older brothers were bossy towards him and sometimes bullied him because he was neither sharp nor streetwise. On many occasions, he not only lacked common sense but was downright stupid.

His predicament was not improved by the fact that he was the favourite child of his tough, domineering, strong-willed mother who contributed dedicatedly to the criminal community. Indeed, she always carried a silver-plated Smith and Wesson under her jacket and used it liberally, whenever she felt it safe to do so.

When a criminal acted for someone who wanted

an enemy shot, he would approach the brothers and their ruthless mother. They negotiated with their client in a rough, unfrequented pub, called The Sawdust, whose landlord was a friend of the family.

Kelvin, Alan and Olive discussed the proposed contract in private, once the request was made. They deliberately excluded Eddy from their negotiations because of his clumsy, blundering nature, and propensity to make crass, deal-busting remarks.

It was Olive who made the decisions about shooting enemies of client contacts, and her older sons never disagreed with her. Their combined attitude was invariably the same.

"Ow, give it to Eddy. He ought to be man enough to do that kind of job, now. The rest of the work should be left to people with brains. It doesn't take brains to pump a few bullets into a bleeding nuisance's body. I love my baby to pieces and all that, but he's too thick for words."

"Mother's right," said Kelvin. "Me and Alan've got a job on tonight, luring a bloke off the streets and impaling his hands on a billiard table, for being a troublemaker in one of our clubs. That's a job to be done, keeping your wits about you, all right. Imagine a berk like Eddy trying to do it."

The three boys shared in common the unbroken worship of their brutally tough mother, whose coffin would be brought into the church that damp, September afternoon.

One thing that was unique about Olive was that she believed in speaking grammatical and articulate English and raised her sons to do the same, although they all spoke with East End accents. Sometimes, when excited, they would lapse into traditional Cockney grammar, particularly when speaking amongst themselves. When addressing acquaintances and adversaries, they tended on the whole to use the kind of language their mother preferred, which, combined with their East End accents, sounded weird, baffling and distinctly menacing.

The three of them had once seen Olive shoot a drunk dead in a deserted street, because he had made mockery of her dying husband's frailty. Kelvin knelt on the ground and kissed her hand, while the combined smell of fresh blood and gunfire wafted towards them in the gentle westerly breeze.

"Mother, you fought for our family honour like a bloody man!" he cried passionately, "Oh, that you could have brought the bastard down, and others like him, with a beautiful, flash Al Capone mashi!" He jerked his arms theatrically in the air, simulating the use of a machine gun.

Eddy, the family idiot, felt he had to say something as well, to compete with his ever-critical brother. He racked his dulled and shrivelled brain for words. He knelt on the ground like his brother.

"Brave mother, brave mother," he eventually managed to mutter.

"OK, two-year-old, you can get up off the ground now," said Kelvin.

Eddy sat alone in the church, remembering his unsympathetic brothers, whom he hadn't seen since they and their mother had sent him on a shooting job in 1963. He wondered if they were still living in the East End and assumed they were.

He had bungled the 1963 job assigned to him, and left a pitiful, clumsy mess behind him. He had no choice but to go on the run. He crossed the Irish sea and lived in Ireland between 1963 and the time of his mother's death. He had married a wealthy woman and had had a son.

His terror of being found by his bludgeoning brothers, caused him to turn to drink and, after the passage of a few years, he destroyed his liver. It was his liver which obsessed and preoccupied him throughout his waking hours in later years, and distracted him from his family and his fear of his brothers finding him. Instead of abstaining from drink, he drank more in order to drown his preoccupation.

The church was full by 1.45. So popular had the

gutsy Olive Vernon been in the East End, and so admired was her desire for rough justice, that over a hundred extra mourners attended her funeral, and had to pay their respects to her in the graveyard. They knelt in the mud in the rain uncomplainingly, when the prayers were said.

Olive Vernon's coffin was removed from a hearse and carried into the church at 2.00 p.m. It was covered with red roses, for red was her favourite colour. She identified it with blood, fire and revenge.

Nearly every head in the congregation turned as she went by. The occupants of the front pew, Kelvin and Alan, and the second pew, Eddy, his wife Marion, his eight-year-old son, Caspar and the boy's elderly nanny, failed to turn their heads, and looked straight in front of them at the altar.

Marion had never met Olive, but accompanied Eddy through compassion, and her knowledge that he did not have long to live. She considered it correct and proper to bring Caspar with her, since Olive was his grandmother, even if they had never met.

Casper had never attended a funeral before, and Marion decided that the nanny should come as well, in case the boy were traumatized by the sight of a box containing a dead body. Marion knew that the nanny had a more homely and comforting effect on the child in adversity than she did.

The coffin was brought to the front of the church and laid on a pedestal in the aisle near the first two pews. A single red rose fell to the floor while this was happening and was hastily picked up and put back on the coffin by an embarrassed pallbearer.

The parson, known personally by the Vernon family, stood in front of the coffin and folded his hands before him. He had shed his original East End brogue and spoke with a resonant, BBC accent.

"Let us give thanks for the life of Olive Vernon...."

He continued, "We will now sing the first hymn, *From Greenland's Icy Mountains*. I would like to point out to you all, that, though not a religious woman, Olive had a special and particular love for this hymn. It meant a very great deal to her, and the sound of it being sung, brought her comfort, peace and joy."

Kelvin thought the parson was uttering too many words and using ludicrously exaggerated language. He cleared his throat ostentatiously.

The organist played the first few bars to introduce *From Greenland's Icy Mountains*. Even to those who had no particular love for its tune, the music sounded like an elixir, like the first second of a drug addict's initial heroin injection.

The congregation was about to sing. Alan's and Kelvin's heads turned round so abruptly that they almost cricked their necks. They shared an alertness which had been instilled in them by their streetwise lifestyles, and heard better than average.

Other members of the congregation enjoyed reasonable enough hearing to recognize the bleat of a mobile telephone. It made a bizarre, alien noise, competing with Olive Vernon's favourite hymn.

The first few bars of *Für Elise* sounded as if they were being played on a cheap tin whistle, and were heard piping in the background of the hymn. It was apparent that this was coming directly from Eddy Vernon. He showed no signs of embarrassment, but of naked fear, like that on the face of a man whose wife is about to give birth.

He threw open his briefcase, thrust his arm into it, and scratched round in it, trying unsuccessfully to put a stop to *Für Elise*. He turned the briefcase upside down in desperation. The bottle of whisky rolled down the sloping aisle, while his brothers gaped at him in disgust. He seized the mobile telephone, and wrenched its lid open so urgently that he nearly snapped it off. He slapped the instrument to his ear.

"Doc!" he bellowed.

Doctor O'Farrell, Vernon's general practitioner, was sitting behind his leather desk in his

Dublin surgery.

"Please don't shout at me," he said quietly. "It is most distressing."

"I've got to shout! You've got to tell me. I must know, NOW! Have my liver function tests come through yet?"

There was something enigmatic about Vernon's accent. It sounded predominantly like a Southern Irish accent, but it was interspersed with the occasional London East End vowel. His accent gave the impression that he had been born and bred in the East End, but had settled in Ireland where he had probably lived for many years.

The nanny knew about Vernon's drinking and general eccentricity, and was partly sympathetic and partly angry. She dug him sharply in the ribs. "You must try to control yourself, sir. You're in the house of God," she muttered in a strident, crisp, cultured English accent.

Kelvin and Alan thought that Eddy's outburst was designed to attract attention and decided to humiliate him by ignoring him.

"You've got to tell me, Doc. I'm worried about my liver!"

"Calm down, sir. It won't be long now. The results of your tests have just been faxed through from the lab. I have them in front of me."

"Yes! Yes! Is it cirrhosis?"

Dr O'Farrell felt as if a burning knitting needle were being pushed into his ear. He held the receiver at the end of his outstretched arm.

"I fear it is, sir."

"Oh, my God! Oh, sweet Christ!"

The parson came quietly over to Vernon. The hymn was long and was still being sung. The louder Vernon's shouting became, the more robustly the congregation sang.

"Will you be quiet, please," said the parson.

Vernon ignored him.

"What does that mean, Doc?"

"Do, please try to stay calm, sir. Your alanine transferase is severely raised. So is your aspartate transaminase. Your gamma GT is highly elevated at over 1000. In short, your liver is beyond repair."

"Oh, God, I can't stand it!"

"Stay calm, now. That way I'll stay calm. Your gamma GT has risen dramatically, since my colleague treated you in hospital some months ago."

"What's the normal reference range for gamma GT, Doc?" screamed Vernon, while occupants in the pew behind him, prodded him in the back.

"5-35. Would you mind turning the music down."

"I can't turn the bloody music down. I'm out on a funeral!" shrieked Vernon.

"Oh, I see," said O'Farrell in a baffled tone,

11

adding angrily, "Your liver is a disgusting, thundering disgrace. You should be ashamed of yourself. I don't mind saying so, sir."

"My liver was always good before I started drinking, Doc."

"Yes, sir. Your liver was once as clean as freshly fallen snow on the steppes of Mother Russia."

The beleaguered parson approached Vernon a second time.

"If this behaviour continues to be unchanged, I shall have to ask you to leave the church."

Vernon ignored him once more.

"I knew something was badly wrong with my liver, as far back as St Patrick's Day. March 17th, that is."

"As an Irishman, I do know that St Patrick's Day is on March 17th," said Dr O'Farrell patiently. "What happened to you on that day?"

"I was sick into an IRA fund-raising bucket!" bellowed Vernon.

Kelvin was livid. He found it unforgivable that his mother's favourite son should be shouting at a doctor on a mobile telephone at her funeral, during her favourite hymn.

He turned round and prodded him in the stomach with his umbrella.

"Shut your bleeding hole!"

"For God's sake, show some compassion. I'm worried sick about my liver," said Vernon, his voice still raised.

"I'm not interested in your blasted, bloody liver. You can't bring a turned on mobile 'phone to your mother's funeral. Turn the bastard off!"

Vernon even ignored the brother whom he had once feared most.

"Any chance of a liver transplant, Doc?"

Kelvin prodded Alan in the ribs and clicked his fingers, something he had done on innumerable occasions in his life when he had wanted someone killed.

The two brothers left their pew and strode to the pew behind them. They grabbed their brother by each arm and dragged him out of the church, into the graveyard. They appeared oblivious of the risk of the outdoor mourners witnessing their proposed act of violence.

Eddy astonished his brothers by failing to resist them. He knew he was dying and preferred to be murdered rather than suffer a painful, lingering death.

The three men reached the gates of the huge cemetery after a ten minute walk. Kelvin and Alan took Eddy across a narrow road and into a deserted side street.

"We're going to kill you, Eddy," said Kelvin.

"You betrayed the lot of us and went to live in Ireland, didn't you?"

"How do you know I've been living in Ireland?" asked Eddy in a disinterested tone.

"We can tell by your horrible accent. We were going to kill you anyway, even if you hadn't done what you did in the church."

"I don't care if you do kill me. I'm not afraid of death."

"Maybe not," said Kelvin laughing, "but you're not going to like our methods of dispatching you into the next world. He's not going to like it one bit, is he Alan?"

"Not one iota, Kelv."

The brothers removed their jackets. They lifted Eddy a foot from the ground and smashed his head against a concrete wall, until his brain protruded from his skull.

Neither Kelvin nor Alan spoke. They put their jackets on, walked back to the church and returned to their pew, after bowing to their mother's coffin.

Eddy had reached the age of fifteen. His brothers took him to pubs where the family was unknown, and made every effort they could to teach him to terrify others, simply by the use of eye contact, a soft voice and a gentle touch of the arm.

The three brothers were walking down a West

End street towards a crowded, rowdy pub one Saturday night.

This was one of the few occasions when Kelvin treated Eddy humanely. He longed to emulate the brothers who were always bullying him and his spirits soared when Kelvin put his arm round him.

"Let's go in now, Eddy, my lad. All you have to do is watch me carefully and hear me speak. There's a full-length mirror behind the bar so you'll see every gesture I make. Then we'll go to another pub where you'll copy me. Me and Alan'll teach you that the only way to get others to obey and respect you is to scare them to death. Right, Al?"

"Right, Kelv."

"When people are afraid of you, you can do anything in the world. You can even rule the world. Just remember that, little brother."

"I'll remember, Kelvin."

"Good lad. We'll go up to the bar."

It was a Saturday night and the queue waiting at the bar was exceptionally long. The situation was not helped by the fact that several customers were still standing at the bar after buying their drinks, adding to the length of the queue.

Kelvin took Eddy aside.

"OK, little brother, here's your first lesson so take it in. Look at the bar and tell me who's annoying you."

"Sorry, Kelvin. I don't understand. Annoying me in what way?"

"Look sharp, stupid! Use your eyes. Scan every bastard standing in the queue. Some sons of bitches are slowing the movement of the queue down. Point them out to me and Alan."

"Oh, sorry, Kelvin. I know who you mean. It's the people who are still standing in the queue, talking to the landlord, after buying their drinks."

"Right, lad. Now I'll tell you how to deal with one of them. I'm going over to the very thin bloke drinking over there, wearing a black bomber jacket.

"Take in how I look at him. Watch in the mirror. I won't look at his eyes. I'll look at his eyebrows. For some reason, that scares people. They think you're looking at their eyes but they find you're not. That confuses them and makes them think you're going to hurt them.

"While you're doing that, you hold them lightly by the back of one of their arms. You don't squeeze."

"Why, Kelvin?"

"Because the fear of being squeezed in that area is far worse than the pain of being squeezed. Put it this way, lad. Imagine an office worker living in fear, year after year, that his boss is going to sack him. Then, after ten years, his boss actually does sack him. He feels as if a bloody great weight has been lifted from his shoulders. Fear of a thing is worse than the thing itself.

"The next thing, and this is the most important, is your speech. You speak very quietly, just loud enough to be heard. It's your words that count. They must be menacing. A quiet voice is far more terrifying than a shout because, in the back of his head, the bloke who hears a quiet voice, fears he will hear a shout which would embarrass him in front of others. Have you taken all this in?"

"Yes."

"Right. What are the three things you do to a person if you want them out of your way? I don't mean dead. I mean in another place."

"Look at the eyebrows. Touch under the arm. Speak quietly, but use strong language."

"Good lad. We'll make a gangster of you yet, won't we, Alan?"

"Right, Kelv."

"Now, I'm going to show you," said Kelvin. "Don't take your eyes off me."

Kelvin went over to the bar and approached the man in the black jacket, who was drinking one glass of Baccardi and Coke after another.

"Can I have a word?" he said in a voice scarcely above a whisper.

"Yeah. What's up?"

Kelvin looked briefly at the man's eyes and then

focused his piercing stare on his eyebrows. The man was no smaller than Kelvin but a wave of naked fear went through him. Kelvin sensed this and to add to his attack, he held him by the back of his right arm without applying any pressure on his flesh.

The man drained his third glass in an attempt to dispel his fear. He felt like a small, frail animal in the clutches of a much bigger, fiercer animal.

"What's the matter, mate? Did I say something I oughtn't to, some other time?"

Kelvin leant forward so that his face was two inches away from that of his adversary. His voice was as silent as the grave.

"You've no business standing in this queue, when you're drinking one after another. You're holding people up. Me and my mates don't tolerate selfish manners. Be a good boy and shift your butt, so as we don't have to give you a good sorting in the street. Because that's what we'll have to do if you don't move, just so as you don't do it again."

The terrified man ran backwards. Kelvin pinched him on the cheek with mock affection and gave him a bogus smile.

"Of course, I knew you'd see sense in the end, laddie. Beatings up ain't nice things. Never 'ave been, 'ave they?"

Eddy and Alan had been standing behind Kelvin

throughout the incident. Kelvin turned to his pupil.

"Did you take all that in, eh?"

"Yes, but you never told me about the smile at the end."

"Doesn't matter. You can add that, too. It's a good touch. Now, we'll wait in the queue for drinks."

The brothers stood at the end of the queue. There was no movement further along the queue, once the customers in front were given drinks. The barman remained in one place, talking to customers at the head of the queue.

The Vernons waited for an hour and there was no sign of the queue diminishing. Kelvin's native astuteness told him that the barman was deliberately avoiding his end of the queue, and assumed this was because neither he nor his brothers, were regulars. Closing time was due within half an hour, which meant that the Vernons would be sent away, frustrated and thirsty.

"Kelvin?" said Eddy in a desperate attempt to please the brother he looked up to and feared most.

"I'm still here, lad. So's Alan."

"I've got an idea."

"What idea, lad?"

"I've been watching that barman all along. He hates us. Can I go up to him and copy your methods of making people afraid?"

"I like the courage you're showing, but this is going to be quite a big job. I was thinking of doing it, myself. I don't even think Alan's up to it. Are you, Alan?"

"Nah. It's hot in here and I've got my migraine coming on."

"Oh, please, Kelvin," said Eddy. "I know I'll get it right."

"All right, lad, but you'll have to do the job properly or else, I'll give you a right thrashing."

Eddy no longer felt as timid as he usually did when under Kelvin's scrutiny. He told himself he was going to get it right and make his brother proud of him. He longed to hear Kelvin's words of praise, so seldom uttered, and feel his arm on his shoulder.

He walked towards the barman, whose face was purple due to excessive alcohol consumption over the years. He was laughing raucously and cracking dirty jokes while talking to his regulars.

He saw Eddy quietly approaching him, and looked at him with disdain.

"How old are yer, boy?" he asked, his speech slurred.

Eddy leaned towards him until their faces were six inches apart. He made a superhuman effort not to gag on smelling the barman's foul breath.

"Twenty next month, if you really want to know."

He continued to stare at the barman. He had temporarily forgotten the eye contact rule. He then fixed his eyes on the barman's eyebrows and continued his hostile stare.

"I'd like a word with you, barman," he said in the tone of voice he'd been taught to use.

The barman looked alarmed.

"Oh?" he said.

"Me and my mates were standing at the end of this queue for an hour. You knew we were there but you were too rude to serve us. We don't like filthy manners and when people show them, we take them out and sort them." He was unable to avoid speaking without a stammer.

The barman was just about to ask Eddy to leave, but Eddy held him under the arm, still focusing his eyes on his eyebrows.

"I haven't quite finished yet, gov'nor."

"I do wish you'd go away. I don't like your manner."

Eddy failed to carry out Kelvin's instructions. Instead of holding the barman's arm, he closed his fingers on it in a vice-like grip, causing him to scream.

"How would you like a carload of the boys?" he said, his stammer much more pronounced.

Kelvin came over to speak to his brother.

"All right, Ed, it's time to go home. Alan's not

feeling too good."

"Was I OK, Kelvin?"

"I'll tell you in the street. Come on."

Eddy expected unquestioning praise from his brother whom he had tried so hard to please and emulate.

"Well, Kelv?"

"Part of what you did was promising. I can't say any more than that. You failed to do as you were told. I said you were only to hold that man's arm, to frighten him, not to clutch it and dispel his fear, through making him feel what the pain was like. Incidentally, where did you hear that expression, 'How would you like a carload of the boys?'"

"At the flicks. Good. Isn't it?"

"I don't care whether you think it's good or not. It's not what I told you to say. Not only that, you were at fault with the eye contact, although you corrected it towards the end, when it was too late. I told you to look at your opponent's eyebrows, not his bloody hairline!"

"Don't be too hard on me. It was my first try."

"So what? You saw me, didn't you? You heard me. You watched me. You told me all the things I'd done, after I'd done them and you got everything right. After you'd seen me, you begged me to let you copy me on someone else. You disobeyed my

22

orders and you went your own sweet way. No wonder everyone says you're stupid!"

Eddy's pride prevented him from wishing to emulate his brother any more that night. Kelvin's words had hurt him beyond endurance. He blinked back his tears on the underground train home, and decided to be co-operative towards Kelvin, without expecting affection or praise, and to do whatever he was asked to do, for his mother's sake. It was she who controlled the family and its activities and not his brother.

Olive was sitting in the living room in her tiny, but immaculately clean house. Her stockinged feet rested on a stool, quilted by her own hand. She was working on her crochet, her tongue protruding in concentration, when her sons silently entered the house, assuming she had gone to bed. She raised her head and smiled with relief, knowing that they hadn't brushed with the Law.

"Hullo, my bunny rabbits. I was wondering what had happened to you. You're ever so late back."

"It's OK, Mother," said Kelvin. "We was trying, I mean we were trying to teach little dumb Eddy a few tricks."

"Oh? How did you get on?"

"How do you expect, Mother? He's a right dozy git. He can't remember anything. He can't seem to do what he's told."

Olive continued to work on her crochet.

"Sometimes, you're a bit cruel, Kelvin. You're always putting him down. He's your kid brother. He's my baby. You don't give him a chance, do you?"

"Baby's certainly the operative word, Mother. You'd never think he was fifteen. He's got the brains of an eight-year-old, haven't you, you stammering little sissy?"

"You're not helping the family, Kelvin," said Olive. "To work as a team, we've got to work in harmony. That can't happen if you're not prepared to be nice to him. You'll have him walking out one day, if you go on treating him like mud. I'm running things and you take orders from me. Off you go to bed, and you, Alan. Eddy, you stay with me a while. I want to talk to you."

"Oh God, Mother!" said Kelvin.

The mother leant forward in her chair and pointed her crochet hook at her eldest son, holding it like a gun.

"Is there something wrong with your hearing, Kelvin? I told you and Alan to go to bed. Kindly obey my orders and get out!"

"It's all right, Mother. Me and Alan'll go up if that's what you want."

Eddy knelt at his mother's feet and

burst into tears.

"I tried so hard, Mother. I did my best." For the first time in his life, he noticed how striking his mother was, with her classical features, liquid grey eyes and her black hair crossing the top of her head in a plait.

Olive got up. Eddy thought she was about to throw her arms round him and comfort him. Instead, she slapped his face.

"No wonder Kelvin gets cross with you, you unmanly, whimpering brat," she said in a strange, shouting whisper. "Kneeling down in front of me and blubbing, aged fifteen. You ought to be ashamed of yourself. You're not a boy any longer. You're a man, and by God, you'll behave like one.

"Ask not what this family can do for you, but what you can do for this family! If you're not prepared to work with us as a team, to fight in this brutal world, you can get out of here and go straight, for all I care. If you can't pull your weight, you're not welcome here. We don't carry slackers. First, you take orders from me, and if I'm not there, you do as Kelvin tells you. Do you understand?"

"Yes, Mother."

"Good. It's late. You'd better go to bed. Kiss me goodnight."

Eddy obeyed. He felt indescribably confused.

25

"Do you still love your mother?" asked Olive.

"Yes, I do, Mother. Good night."

"Goodnight, my baby."

The family sat down to breakfast at 9.00 the next morning, and behaved as if the accumulative unpleasantness the night before had never occurred. Olive poured out the tea. Her only verbal output was a remark about the continuing inclement weather which had made her irritable of late.

Kelvin was sitting with his feet on the table, cramming bread, butter and jam into his mouth, turning over the pages of an old edition of *The Daily Sketch*.

"Kelvin," said Olive.

"Yes, Mother?"

"Get your feet off the table this instant, and put that paper down. It's very rude to read at meals, and it's even ruder to put your feet up. Anyone would think you'd learned your manners in a sewer."

Kelvin removed his feet hurriedly. He laid the newspaper down, folded it up and put it gently under the table.

"I'm ever so sorry, Mother," he said quietly. "I wasn't thinking."

"No. You weren't thinking, were you? Nor were you setting an example to Eddy."

"Oh, yes, little Eddy," muttered Kelvin.

"Just you shut up! You were fifteen once. I'm not above pouring hot tea over you, either."

There was a long silence. Eddy tried to blink back his tears. He lowered his head and slowly spread butter onto his bread.

"What are you doing today, boys?" asked Olive. "How are you going to make yourselves useful, eh?"

Kelvin felt humbled after his mother's robust admonishment.

"Well, me and Alan were ..."

"Alan and I," corrected Olive. "No-one would have thought I'd taught you any grammar."

"Oh, come, Mother. I did say I was sorry for being rude."

"All right, all right. What are your plans?"

"Alan and I were thinking of taking Eddy out and teaching him how to go on the tweedle."

"Ah, yes, the tweedle. That's the first trick my Dad ever taught me. It's nice and easy. As long as Eddy keeps his head, he'd be quite good at it."

"What's the tweedle, Mother?" asked Eddy.

"I'll tell you. First you go into Woolworth's where you buy a cheap brass ring for half a crown. Then you go into a fancy jeweller's, and pick out an identical ring in the window, except it will be gold and worth a hundred pounds or more. You go into the shop and someone will ask if they can help you.

"You lead them to the gold ring, and say you want to buy your mother a birthday present, as her wedding ring was ripped off her finger by a thief in a deserted street. Make yourself look wistful when you say this.

"Then, either Kelvin or Alan will distract the assistant and you will swap the rings. You put the pricy one in your pocket and ask for the price of the cheap one. When you're told the price, you say, 'sorry, I can't afford it. Thanks for your help, anyway,' and leave. Will you do that, Eddy? It will keep the family alive for a week or two."

"Yes. I'll do it, Mother."

As the boys were leaving the house, Olive took Kelvin aside.

"Eddy's so keen to help us all. Promise me you won't be nasty to him? He really looks up to you. Not only that, we've got to keep the family together. That way, we'll hit the big time one day."

"I'll do whatever you say, Mother. I know I get impatient with him when he cocks things up, but I promise I won't be nasty to him."

"Tick him off if he's stupid, but don't keep calling him "little Eddy" when it's not necessary. It's hurtful to him, as well as damaging to the family."

"I did give you my word, Mother."

The tweedle was successful. Eddy did as he was

told, and even rustled up some tears, when telling the jeweller's assistant that his mother had been robbed of her wedding ring.

Kelvin took the stolen ring to another jeweller's a long way from the first jeweller. He sold the stolen ring for a hundred and fifty pounds, while his brothers waited for him outside. The three of them made their way home from the West End on the underground.

"How much did it fetch, Kelvin?" asked Eddy.

"A hundred and fifty pounds. You did well today. I know Mother will be pleased."

Olive was indeed pleased, but she was not nearly as happy as Eddy, because his elder brother had told him he had done well. He began to change.

He remained absent-minded, but his self-confidence gradually increased. He grew tougher and less dependent on the occasional praise from his family, which he had once revelled in.

The family sat down for their meal at 6.00 one evening. They were too exhausted to speak. It was not until they had finished eating, that Olive got up and banged her fist on the table.

"I'm going to make contract killers of you all, one day! It's going to be rags to riches for the lot of us. We're going to be millionaires. We won't have to lurk about in these stinking backstreets any more."

Her sons said nothing, and smiled radiantly at their mother. They went upstairs to bed. Their mother slept downstairs in her chair.

Claude and Sally Bamber lived in a grand, Queen Anne house outside Farnham, in Surrey's stockbroker belt. Sally was a plump, loose-looking buxom blonde. Bamber was tall, thin and bald, of unprepossessing appearance and boundless wealth.

They had no children because Sally was infertile. She had wanted children and was lonely and frustrated at times, but she felt liberated, because she had no cause for the tedious intricacies of birth control. She took advantage of her medical condition and revelled in promiscuity.

Bamber commuted to the City each day, wearing a pin stripe suit and bowler hat, looking unattractive, boring and stiff. Sally received lovers.

Indeed, her sex-drive was so overpowering that she was careless in her activities. She ignored the presence of Mrs Blackstock, her housekeeper, who was in all day, and who could hear every word and shout which passed between her mistress and her many male visitors in the matrimonial bedroom.

It was fortunate for Sally that Mrs Blackstock found the situation amusing, and refrained from telling Bamber what was happening during his absence.

The Bambers came from different social classes. Claude was raised in a wealthy family. His father and grandfather were rich landowners. Claude had no need to work for a living, and only chose to work in the City to satisfy his work ethic.

Sally came from a working class background, and obtained exceptional secretarial skills in her last year at a grammar school in South London.

She was intellectually sharp and ambitious, despite her loose-looking, wench-like appearance. She was ashamed of her humble origins, and was determined to improve her social status. She qualified with higher typing and shorthand speeds than anyone in her class, which enabled her to work to a standard required by top executives.

Bamber was more than just a stockbroker, and was referred to as such for the sake of simplicity. He started as a stockbroker, and later served as a personal adviser to politicians, high court judges, publishers and newspaper proprietors, as well as their families.

The management in Bamber's London offices advertised for a personal assistant. There were seventeen applicants, all of whom were interviewed by Bamber personally, before having to submit to a typing, shorthand and I.Q. test.

Not only did Bamber's tastes in women veer towards heavily made-up faces and stiletto heels. He was also impressed by the cultured accent Sally had adopted, her articulate manner and her knowledge of high finance, much of which she had gained from her secretarial training.

He overlooked the fact that she had never worked before. When one of his personnel officers tested her, and found her typing and shorthand speeds to be seventy and a hundred and twenty-five, he appointed her.

They worked together for five years. Sally had managed to save a handsome sum, half of which she gave to her invalid mother in Lewisham. She told Bamber that she was becoming bored with working as his personal assistant, and that she wanted to settle down and raise a family.

He realized he would have to find another personal assistant, possibly with fewer skills, but he felt comfortable with Sally and decided to propose to her. Life-long security was of paramount importance to her and she accepted. After their honeymoon in the West Indies, she moved into his Queen Anne house in Surrey.

As a husband, he was different from an employer. At least as an employee, she felt the satisfaction of impressing him by the quality of her work, without her having to make conversation to him.

It was just before the end of the year, 1962. Sally had been excited and elated at that time. She had been rivetted by the Cuban crisis and for some weeks, she had been overjoyed by its outcome.

Her euphoria was short-lived, however. It took

her only a few weeks of marriage to realize what an unutterably boring man Bamber was.

Two doctors told her that she was irreparably infertile, which distressed and frustrated her, particularly as she had nothing to do. She decided she was faced with two alternatives, either to leave her husband and find work away from the house, or to take lovers. She decided upon the latter.

Bamber found a less capable personal assistant, which meant he had to work much harder. Most nights, he failed to come home until 10.00 p.m. He liked Sally to cook him a gourmet dinner, when she would have preferred to be in bed, reading a book at that time.

He was always worn out, and his conversation was so limited and devoid of interest, that there were times when he reduced her to tears of abject boredom. She would have been happier, had he not spoken at all.

The tireder Bamber was, the more he talked in a monotonous, rambling manner, unaware of what he was saying. His conversation caused any tormented listener to feel as if a nail were being hammered into the back of his neck in slow motion.

Sally had spent the afternoon being satiated by a lover and was initially perkier on her husband's homecoming.

"How was your day, dear?" she forced herself

to ask him, feeling mischievously contented by her deceit of a man she was beginning to despise.

"The same sort of day as I usually have. It rained most of the way to London and most of the way back, although I was just able to see the sun coming out from behind a cloud, ten minutes before I was due to get off the London-bound train," he said, speaking on the same note, with increasing rapidity.

"Ah, yes," said Sally.

"I'm not nearly through yet, dear. I've so many other things to tell you."

"Oh, dear."

He ignored her mild criticism and continued.

"The weather forecast had predicted a sunny but essentially cold day. They never get it right."

"Haven't you got anything else to talk about, besides the weather?"

"Oh, yes, plenty, dear. I couldn't get a seat on the train on the way to London. I had to stand in the corridor, but at least I had a chance to have a long talk with a nice old Scotsman called Bill Campbell. He and I often have to stand. We've become very good friends. We've always got something to talk about."

"Do you and he just stand there, talking about the weather, all the way to London and back?"

"Sometimes, we do. It's an interesting subject,

the weather."

"I can't say I share your opinion. Where does your friend work?"

"He's retired. He goes to London every day and does hospital voluntary work."

"That's nice of him, isn't it?" said Sally, affably.

"He does it to keep himself sane. His wife's dead," said Bamber.

There was a pause of about ten minutes. Both husband and wife were on the verge of weeping, he with exhaustion, she with a yearning for another sexual and conversationally stimulating encounter, with any man other than her husband.

"There's a man on the train who reads a French grammar book. I presume he is learning French," said Bamber.

"It would appear so, wouldn't it?"

"I can't remember whether you speak French or not. Do you speak it?"

"No."

"The man learning French had to stand in the corridor, too," rambled Bamber. "Even the corridor was crowded, so much so that he was leaning against me. He was muttering irregular verbs under his breath. My French isn't too good, I'm bound to say. The most difficult thing about the language is the difference between the verbs coming after *avoir* and the ones coming after *être*."

Sally said nothing. She went to the kitchen and brought a steaming plate of mussels into the dining room, and put it down on the table. Bamber tucked his napkin into his collar and ate the mussels greedily, making sucking noises as he did so. He threw the shells onto the table, and occasionally onto the floor, while Sally turned her head away, nauseated.

"Who the hell's going to pick those up? For someone of your breeding, your table manners are nothing short of revolting," she remarked.

He appeared not to hear her.

"He was there yesterday, and the day before that. In fact, he's been there every day for some time."

"Who has?"

"The man."

"What man, dear?"

"The man reading the French grammar book."

"Oh, God, we're back on him now, are we?"

"That's right. He was wearing a brown jacket, today. Last week, he wore a green jacket. Same man. Same book. On wet days, he brings an umbrella with him. I suppose that would stand to reason. What do you think?"

"I don't know how much longer I'm going to be able to put up with this, Claude," said Sally. "Your conversation is getting duller and duller every day. I'd prefer it if you said nothing at all, unless you've got something important or interesting to say. I'm going up, now. Mrs Blackstock will do the dishes in the morning."

"Oh, you're going up, are you? I've suddenly thought of something you might like to hear." He paused, either as if about to divulge a naughty secret, or as if he wanted to drive her into a rage for his own entertainment.

"Get on with it, Claude."

"There's something I've just thought of. When I was a boy, I didn't like tomatoes at all. Now, I like them very much. I wonder why that is."

She rose to her feet.

"This is simply not interesting, Claude. Goodnight."

"Will you tell me one thing before you go up?"

"What, Claude?"

"Are you having any men in while I'm in London?"

"Wise up, will you, man! What do you think?"

"I don't know. If I did, I wouldn't have asked, would I?"

"Yes, of course I have men in from time to time. Can you imagine how bored I am alone in this house? I have to have something to occupy myself with, while I'm dreading your return and your spine-chillingly boring conversation."

"I don't know when I'm being a bore," he said. " I work very hard and I get worn out. I like to talk in the evenings because I love you, and all I want is someone being here to listen to me. I like to describe the things I see each day."

"Do you think anyone would be remotely interested to hear about the clothing worn by men learning French on trains, elderly Scotsmen visiting hospitals, and want to be subjected to monologues about the bloody weather?"

"You've turned into a cruel, rude woman, Sally," began Bamber. "I am and always have been a gentle, mild-mannered man, but even the most decent man in the world can turn into Hyde overnight. If you kick a friendly Labrador too many times, it will turn into the Hound of the Baskervilles.

"I've been kind to you. I've employed you. I've given you riches and a beautiful house to live in. I work like a navvy to ensure your comfort and enable you to have everything you wish for, because I still love you, despite your insults. In fact, I'm infatuated with you. I'd like to throw you out but I can't because it would break my heart. Now that you confess to taking lovers, I feel myself turning from a man of reason, into a monster."

"What's that supposed to mean?" asked Sally.

He walked close to her without touching her. She could smell the garlic from the mussels on his breath which was already stale.

"I'd never hurt you, Sally. My love for you, despite your unkindness, is too strong for that, but if I ever find you in the presence of another man, I shall not hesitate to kill him or have him killed."

"How could you catch me if you're in London when I see men?"

"Don't be too sure. I could come back here during the day at any time."

"You wouldn't be strong enough to kill a man."

"Not at this moment, I wouldn't. Nor would a friendly Labrador, but that doesn't mean the Hound of the Baskervilles wouldn't. One could turn into the other very, very quickly.

"It would never be you I'd hurt. I wouldn't be capable, but I'd stop at nothing to bring about the death of any man daring to make love to you. You are mine, mine to have and mine to hold, and no-one in the world is ever going to take you from me, however much you might want to leave me."

Sally walked away from him as she wished to go to bed. She made a decision to be more discreet as the sight of blood was abhorrent to her. As she left the room, awash with fear, she turned to her husband in a spirit of palpably bogus boldness.

"I'll leave you whenever I feel like it!" she

shouted. "I'll leave this part of the world, get a job somewhere and settle down with a man of my choice when the time comes. And it will be an interesting man that I choose, not a paralysing bore like you. Try and stop me!"

Once he was alone in the kitchen, Bamber burst into tears, brought on by a conflict of besotted love for his wife and a desire for violent revenge, which he knew she believed to be no more than an empty threat.

It was January 1963 and the whole of England was blanketed by snow. As the weeks passed by, Sally had become more discriminating in her selection of lovers. There were days when she abstained completely from carnal activity.

She cultivated a liking for films and watched them at least once a week. She went to a cinema in Farnham which showed a different film every few days. It was not far from her house. She drove there in Bamber's car which she left in the cinema carpark.

If she failed to understand the plot of the film or was unable to hear what a character said, she was not too shy to ask a stranger sitting next to her to explain and interpret for her.

She had gone to see an incomprehensible film entitled *The List of Adrian Messanger*, a detective film in which the characters continuously changed their identities, by disguising themselves as other characters with the use of masks.

She noticed a large, moustachiod, muscular man in the seat next to her, but made no observation of his features. He was sitting motionless, concentrating on the film. She dug the man sharply in the ribs.

"What did he way? Sorry, I can't understand American accents."

"He said ..." replied the man, but because of the loudness of the voices on the screen, she failed to hear the end of his sentence.

"Sorry. I didn't hear what *you* said," she said.

"What did you say?"

"I want to know what that man said about thirty seconds ago. Also, who's the man he's just been speaking to?"

A woman sitting in front of them, turned round and shushed them.

"I'm afraid I don't know."

"You don't know?"

"No. This is a dreadful film. I can't follow what's going on, at all."

"I think it's a terrible film, as well," she said, ignoring the repeated request for silence from the woman in the row in front.

She suddenly looked closely at the man. His hair

was dark brown and thick, and his profile was aquiline. He was about thirty and attractive. His breath smelt of cigar smoke and reminded her of the many lovers she had had, who liked cigars.

"Let's get up and leave," she said.

She rose to her feet and walked towards the EXIT sign. He followed her. He assumed what she wanted on observing her peroxide hair, heavy make-up and wench-like appearance, He was attracted by her keenness to lead the way, rather than be led, which had been the case in the myriad of other women he had associated with.

He looked at her, expecting her to take the initiative.

"There's a café not far from here that I know," she said. "We'll go there and discuss the film, and agree how appallingly bad it was. We'll have tea. After that, we might go back to the cinema and ask for our money back."

"I must say, I find that awfully witty," said the man, who spoke with a heavy public school accent.

"I'm an awfully witty person," she said, adding, "You know what I want us to do after we've been back to the cinema to get refunded, don't you?"

"Yes, by God!" he replied, his voice raised and his public school accent even more pronounced. As he spoke, he raised his right leg and slapped his thigh, in the way Hitler did when he heard that

Austria had been taken. "Ben Earnshaw's my name. What's yours, young lady?"

She took him by the arm and leant against him, as if she had been married to him for twenty years.

"I'm Sally Bamber," she said.

The place she led him to was not a café, but an old-fashioned tea house, with a bay window, overlooking a narrow street. As they went in, she called to a waitress, wearing a black dress and a white apron, edged with lace. The waitress turned towards her.

"Good afternoon, Mrs Bamber."

"Hullo, Avril. The gentleman and I wish to sit at the table by the window."

"Certainly. What will you have, today?"

"The same as I always have when I come in here. A pot of tea with hot muffins and honey."

"And the gentleman?"

"He will be having the same."

Earnshaw's attraction to Sally increased. He had had a crush on a matron at Eton, and had a penchant for bossy, domineering women. He was only capable of sexual arousal when being pushed around by them, particularly if they had dyed hair and looked rather common.

Sally held his hand tightly under the table, and manipulated his aristocratic, tapering fingers like a masseuse. Neither spoke until after they had started their tea.

"You've got nice hands," she said. "They're hardly a labourer's hands. You don't work, do you?"

"How do you know?"

"If you had a job, you wouldn't be able to go to the cinema in the afternoons, would you?"

"I find your manner and the freshness of your questions exciting. Most of the women I've met are shy and docile. No. I don't work. I don't have to. My father was very rich. He was a Brigadier in the Guards. I was in the Army for a short time. I was a Lieutenant. My father's dead, now. So's my mother. They left me rather a nice house in Greenhill Lane, the other side of the woods."

"Do you live alone?"

"Yes. Except for my housekeeper."

"What do you do with your time, besides go to the cinema?"

"I've got a lot of friends in Farnham, mostly the children of my father's friends. Surely, you don't want me to bore you with a résumé of what I do from waking up time until bed-time."

She pulled him gently by the tie.

"Oh, yes, I do."

"All right, I'll tell you, but as soon as you get bored, you're to tell me to stop."

"I won't get bored. Get on with it."

"My housekeeper calls me at 11.00 a.m. when she brings me breakfast. It takes me about an hour and a half to get up. I go to my club where I meet my friends for lunch. They're rich and don't have to work either. Sometimes, we play backgammon and billiards after lunch. That's if I don't go to the cinema."

"You enjoy going to the cinema, don't you? We have that in common. What sort of films do you like?"

"Well, I certainly don't like mushy romances."

"I wasn't asking you what you didn't like. I was asking you what you liked," she said, as she poured more tea into the two empty cups.

"God, I liked the way you said that! Your pert, peremptory manner really does something to me. The films I like are Westerns, who-dunnits and adventure films in general. Alfred Hitchcock's my favourite. What about you?"

"I like films with a lot of sex in them. X-films."

"Oh? Are you married?"

"Yes, but there's nothing going between me and my husband. He's the most boring man I've ever known. All he talks about is the weather. I have extra-marital affairs to keep myself sane. That's why I'll be coming to your house in Greenhill Lane after tea."

"Wow!" exclaimed Earnshaw.

"I want to know more about you. Where did you go to school?"

"Eton. The walls of my room were covered with semi-naked photographs of a woman who looked rather like you. So did the house matron. She was fierce with a loud, commanding voice. I'd have given anything to lie on her."

"Well, you'll soon be lying on me if I've got anything to do with it, won't you, you fabulous hulk?"

"Oh, God Almighty, yes!"

Avril, the waitress, came over and tapped Earnshaw on the shoulder.

"May I have a word, sir?"

"Why, yes. What can I do for you?"

"I'm afraid your conversation has taken a turn for the vulgar, sir. It's upsetting my other customers. Would you mind keeping your voice down."

"Oh, yes, certainly. I'm most awfully sorry. It won't happen again."

"Kindly see that it doesn't."

They walked back to the cinema carpark and scrambled urgently into Bamber's car.

"Direct me to your house, Ben," Sally commanded.

"Were you ever in the Wrens?"

"No. Why?"

"You've got that sort of aura about you."

She turned on the ignition and revved up the engine.

"Come on. Show me the way."

"Third left. Second right. Through two sets of traffic lights. Straight on till you get to a country road. Through the woods. Out the other side. Second left. Hurry!"

He felt a sharp pain in his chest and his breathing became laboured. As he looked at his peroxide blonde companion's pretty profile, it worsened. He feared he was about to have a heart attack and die before consummating his lust.

She stopped abruptly outside his house, churning up the snow and gravel in the drive. They got out. He let himself in with his latchkey. The house was a Queen Anne house like the Bambers'. The walls of the hall were covered with mildly pornographic drawings.

Two swing doors led to a large dining room, its walls panelled with dark oak. The long, rectangular table and upright chairs surrounding it, were seventeenth century. A wall to wall window looked onto a two acre garden, with a steeply sloping lawn, ending in a pretty, evergreen wood.

Earnshaw led Sally into the dining room, with his arm round her waist. He was angry, and surprised to find his housekeeper, Mrs Turner, still polishing the table, when she was supposed to go off duty, once he went to his club for lunch.

"I say, Mrs Turner, you've stayed a bit late, haven't you?" he said irritably.

"Sorry, sir. I wasn't feeling too well, so I had a rest and came back to finish my work afterwards."

"I see. Well, would you mind awfully, stopping whatever you're doing? I'd like you to leave the premises, now. Come back tomorrow."

Mrs Turner looked baffled. She picked up her dusters and tin of polish, and stared sheepishly at her employer.

"Yes. I'll be on my way straight away, sir. I'm sorry I was still here when you came back."

"All right, all right. Just go, will you!"

Mrs Turner ran into the hall and out into the drive. The temperature, for which the winter of 1963 is notorious, was below freezing. She was shrewd enough to know why her employer was angry, and decided to freeze, rather than go back into the house to look for her overcoat and risk the loss of her job.

Sally and Earnshaw waited for the front door to close and threw their arms round each other.

"Going down, yes?" shouted Sally in a staccato voice, which excited Earnshaw so much, that his chest pain returned and his breathing became so laboured, that he thought he was going to die.

She knelt in front of him and stretched out her hands.

"Oh, Mother, help me!" he muttered.

It was not long before he realized he was in love with Sally, as well as being stricken with a lust for her, which was no longer pleasurable but painful.

"We'll go upstairs, now," he said gently.

"Like hell, we won't! We'll use the table. I want it rough, so you'd better give me what I came for!"

They rolled off the table onto the floor, exhausted.

"How long can you stay?" asked Earnshaw.

"The old bore won't be back until 10.00, so to be on the safe side, I'll have to leave at 9.00."

"If you hate him so much and you seem so happy with me, why can't you divorce him?"

"You don't realize how dangerously possessive he is. He knows I've been seeing other men, and he told me that if he found me with a man, he'd kill him outright."

"Rubbish!" said Earnshaw. "Husbands always talk like that if they love their wives."

At 9.00, Sally left Earnshaw with tears in her eyes. She wanted to marry him and divorce her husband. She reversed the car up the sloping drive. As she drove through the woods, she skidded on the ice and ended up in some foliage. However much she revved up the engine, the car failed to move. She got out to seek help.

It was not until 9.45 that someone stopped. Her rescuer was driving a Landrover and had a coil of rope in the back. He was a farmer called Freddie Gladdon and, because he was a public-spirited man, he kept it to pull stranded drivers out of snowdrifts.

Gladdon got out of his Landrover.

"Stuck in the brambles, I see?"

"Yes. Can you help me?"

"Don't see why not. I've got some rope here. I always carry it with me, because so many people need to be towed out of snowdrifts this winter. It's the worst we've ever had."

"Oh, you're too kind!"

"Just leave it to me. I'll tie the rope to the front of your car and have you out in a few seconds. Rev your engine and get into first. I'll go back and do the same."

Gladdon towed the car back onto the road. He undid Sally's end of the rope. She was so flustered about being found out, that she drove off without having the courtesy to thank Gladdon.

She thought she might be at the receiving end of celestial punishment, when she found Bamber standing outside the front door, his arms arrogantly folded and his legs parted. He wasn't wearing an overcoat in the perilously cold weather. She got out of the car and walked towards him, hating him even more vehemently, and no longer afraid of his threats to kill her lover.

"Do you know what the time is?"

"Yes. I'm wearing that rather vulgar watch you gave me. It's 10.30 exactly."

"Where have you been? I've been waiting for my dinner."

"Out in the car. I skidded on some ice. The car wouldn't move. I had to wait in the freezing cold for someone to tow me back onto the road."

"You'd better come indoors. We'll continue this discussion then."

Sally followed Bamber into the hall and took off her overcoat, which she threw defiantly on the floor.

"Why did you take the car out at this hour of night?" he asked.

"I'm over twenty-one, Claude. I have as much ownership of the car as you do, and if I wish to take it out, I shall do so."

"Where did you take it, Sally?"

"I don't see that that's any of your business."

"I haven't had any dinner."

"When you found I was out, you should have made some yourself. There's plenty of food in the fridge."

"I asked you where you took the car."

"What does it matter where I took it? You've just complained that you've had nothing to eat. I've had a terrible time out there. I'm not cooking for you, now. Go and get yourself some bread and cheese."

"Where did you take the car?" shouted Bamber.

'"Go and get yourself some bread and cheese,' I said!"

Their conversation continued its repetitive course until midnight. Sally thought the words "go and get yourself some bread and cheese," would serve as a magic shield, to prevent her from being forced to make a confession.

Bamber's repeated question gave her a migraine. She no longer believed he had either the will or the power to kill one of his rivals, and because of her loathing for him, she decided to hurt him in such a way that he would wish to divorce her and set her free.

"Where did you take the car?" he repeated for the last time.

"I'll tell you where! I took it to visit my lover. I'm having an affair with him. I'm in love with him and I despise you so much that I demand a divorce from you."

He eased her against the wall, his arms on either side of her to prevent her moving. He had done this on a few occasions in the past, and it was a gesture which infuriated her.

"Let me pass!" she shrieked.

He slapped her gently across the face.

"So you'll hit me, will you? Now, I'll divorce you on grounds of knocking me about."

"I have never knocked you about, and you will not divorce me," he said quietly.

"In that case, I'll leave and live with him in sin."

"What's his name, Sally?"

"Do you think me fool enough to tell you that, when you said you'd kill any man having an affair with me?"

"But you didn't believe me."

It was now 1.00 in the morning. The mixture of hatred and exhaustion made Sally feel as if she'd had too much to drink.

"Come on! What's the bastard's name?" said Bamber.

"He's no bastard like you, and his name's Ben Earnshaw," she said recklessly.

They spent the night in separate rooms. Sally slept in the matrimonial bedroom, and Bamber used one of the spare rooms. By 3.00 a.m., he was still unable to sleep. He went down to the drawing room and picked up the telephone directory. He found a lengthy column of Earnshaws covering two pages.

He feared his rival might be ex-directory, and the Earnshaws whose first names began with a B, covered an entire page. He wondered whether Ben might be a nickname, and because he was so depressed by his lack of success, he went over to the drinks tray and poured himself three measures of whisky.

He went back to his chair and took two swigs to steady his nerves. He picked up a magnifying glass, and combed the next dizzying page of Earnshaws. He found the entry he thought he'd been looking for. The name he saw was Lt. Kenneth Francis Benjamin Earnshaw of Greenhill House, Greenhill Lane, Farnham, Surrey, telephone number Farnham 5314. He felt humbled and even angrier on finding that his rival was a man of rank.

He memorized the entry, and scanned the remaining Earnshaws to make sure there were no others with Benjamin among their first names. He slept in his clothes for a few hours. He woke up at 8.00 a.m. and made himself three cups of coffee and several pieces of toast, as he had had nothing to eat since lunch-time the day before.

He rang his office in London and told his personal secretary he was unwell. At 9.00 a.m. Sally continued to sleep happily, and Bamber put on his fur-lined coat, gloves and Siberian hunter's hat, and drove into the centre of Farnham, to the offices of a firm of private detectives called James Buxton and Co.

He rang the bell and an elderly receptionist came to the door.

"Good morning, sir. Come in out of the freezing cold and take a seat. May I take your coat, hat and gloves? You certainly know how to protect yourself from the cold."

Bamber preferred to indulge in interminable monologues himself, but was averse to others doing the same.

"It's all right, thank you. I'm still cold. I wish to make an appointment to see Mr James Buxton. My name's Claude Bamber," he said brusquely.

"You do? Well, you're in luck. He was due to see a client at 10.00 but the client rang up a few minutes ago to say he had 'flu. I'm making coffee. Would you like some?"

"Yes. I could certainly do with some."

"It's 9.45, now. Only another fifteen minutes to go. Mr Buxton's always pleased to see a new client."

At 10.00, the receptionist contacted Buxton on the internal telephone.

"Mr Claude Bamber to see you, sir. Mr Bamber, would you please go on up. It's the first office on the left on the first floor."

Buxton was an unusually large man with big

blue eyes, which never focused on any object for more than a second at a time. He had receding fair hair and wore a thick, grey and white striped suit.

When Bamber entered the room, Buxton rose to his feet and shook his hand. His handshake was almost firm enough to crush his knuckles.

"Mr Claude Bamber, isn't it?"

"Yes. And you are Mr James Buxton."

"That is correct. Please sit down. Then you can tell me what you want me to do for you."

Both men sat down. Buxton was irritated by the fact that Bamber refused to remove any of his outer clothing. His mother had taught him that it was rude not to take one's overcoat off and hang it up on a peg, on entering a building.

"Is my office too cold for you? It is centrally heated, you know," he said with a forced smile.

"Oh, is it?"

"Yes. It is indeed. Are you going to take your coat off or would you prefer to sit here with it on?"

Bamber realized that he had annoyed the man whose help he so desperately wanted.

"I'm so sorry. I wasn't thinking." He rose to his feet and hurriedly took off his overcoat, hat and gloves, which he bundled up and put on the floor by his chair.

"Mr Bamber," began Buxton. "I don't want to sound fussy, and indeed I look forward to our prolonged business association, but I do have rather irritatingly high standards of tidiness and protocol. Would you please pick up that pile of clothing and hang it up neatly on one of the pegs in the corridor."

Bamber's resentment of his wife's infidelity was so overpowering that he obeyed Buxton automatically. He came back into the room and sat down.

"I'm so sorry," he repeated. "It was most absent-minded of me. It won't happen again."

"So, what is the trouble?" asked Buxton, smiling.

"It's my wife. She says she's in love with a certain Lt. Kenneth Francis Benjamin Earnshaw, known simply as Ben Earnshaw. I want both of them tailed, so that I can have grounds for divorcing her."

"First, we will have to find out where this man lives," said Buxton.

"Oh, I know where he lives, all right. He lives at Greenhill House, Greenhill Lane, Farnham, and his telephone number is Farnham 5314."

Buxton felt his irritation rising once more, but as his firm was in debt, and he needed every customer he could get, he forced himself to smile, showing two gold teeth at the back of his mouth.

"It would appear that you have already done

most of my work for me," he said. "Now that you know his address, what else would you like me to do?"

"I'd like you to send someone out to watch the house, wait for them to come out, and get your man to photograph them together. Then I'd be in a position to sue for divorce."

"That can be done very easily," said Buxton. "It would mean my putting my snoopers in Greenhill Lane in shifts, for twelve hours a day, one man at a time. It will be a costly operation but if that is what you want, it can be done.

"I warn you, that because of the weather conditions, people are disinclined to go out much, so it may take a considerable time before one of my men can get the picture you need. It would help if you could give me some idea of what your wife looks like."

"She's blonde and slightly overweight. Her hair is long. Sometimes, she wears it loose. Other times, she takes it back in a ribbon or a slide. She's not pretty but most men would find her sexually attractive. She wears a lot of make-up. I suppose that's the fashion nowadays."

Buxton suddenly looked animated.

"Does she look anything like Marilyn Monroe?"

"No such luck."

"You don't have any idea what the man looks

like, do you?"

"No, I'm afraid not. I should imagine he looks a bit flashy, as I think that's the sort of thing she'd go for," said Bamber, adding, "What are your fees?"

"Not like they used to be, I fear. This is 1963 and our rates have gone up. The fee for the men will be a pound an hour, of which they will keep ten shillings. Consultation costs, including general costs, will amount to thirty pounds a week."

Bamber winced. He could easily afford Buxton's services, but he was concerned about the additional cost of the hitman he intended to hire to kill Earnshaw, an event which would be impossible until the hitman had scrutinized his photograph.

"I'll agree to your costs. I have cash with me and I'll pay you up front to get it off my chest," he said.

"Why, Mr Bamber, that's excellent!" exclaimed Buxton.

As Bamber put his hand in the inside pocket of his jacket, preparing to pay Buxton, the two men were interrupted by someone knocking on the door.

"Come in!" said Buxton angrily.

A man aged about twenty came into the room. He was short and walked with a distracted, shuffling gait, made more pronounced on hearing the firm's manager raising his voice. He had untidy, longish dark hair, parted in the centre, and covering most of his sallow face as if to give him anonymity. He had a dirty green and white sheepskin coat draped over his shoulder, and was carrying a large brown envelope.

"Yes? What is it?" asked Buxton.

"This arrived for you, sir. I was asked to bring it up to you, straight away."

"What do you mean by draping your overcoat over your shoulder like that in here, as if you were spending the day in a betting shop? Hang it up and put it on one of the pegs in the corridor, this instant!"

"Yes, sir. I'm sorry."

"So you should be. And another thing you can do is put a comb through your hair, if you wish to go on working here. You can go, now."

"I'll give you the envelope first, sir."

"Thank you. Now, beat it."

Bamber and Buxton parted amicably. Bamber went home, and found that Sally had left. The only person in the house was Mrs Blackstock.

"I notice Mrs Bamber's not here," said Bamber.

"No. She packed all the belongings she needed, and left in a taxi. She told me she wasn't coming back."

"Did she say where she was going?"

"Yes. To her mother's in Lewisham."

"That certainly isn't true. When did she leave?"
"An hour ago, sir."

Sally arrived at Greenhill House with her belongings. Mrs Turner opened the door.

"I know you. You was here yesterday, wasn't you? Wait here. I'll tell Lt. Earnshaw. He's in his room."

"There's a lady to see you, sir."

"What does she look like?"

"It's the same lady who was here yesterday. She's brought all her things with her."

"Excellent! Send her up to my bedroom, straight away. There's no time like the present, eh, Mrs Turner?" he said vulgarly.

The lovers stayed in bed for three days. They only refrained from carnal activity when Mrs Turner, disgusted by her employer's morals, brought them meals on trays.

They lived in this way for a week. Earnshaw was still besotted by his matronly companion, but had become frustrated with the monotonous arrangement. He suggested taking her to his club, so that he could show off his new buxom acquisition to his friends.

"We must get out, Sally. We need a change of air. There are so many restaurants and pubs I want to show you, and I want to take you to my club."

"I'm afraid to go out, yet," she said. "My husband knows who you are and he really does mean to kill you."

"How does he know who I am?"

"He knows because I gave him your name."

"That was damned silly of you. I'm in the 'phone book. He could come here and find me anyway, whether we go out or not."

"Then there's the problem with the car," said Sally.

"What problem?"

"That bastard left the house and took it with him. I can't use it any more."

"So what? I've got a beautiful brand new Jag in my garage. It's British racing green. You'll love it. It goes a hell of a lot faster than Bamber's rubbishy old bucket."

Their conversation had been taking place in the dining room on their first morning away from Earnshaw's bedroom. They had had breakfast, and had just finished indulging in noisy and brutal carnal activity, on the dining room table, causing crockery and cutlery to crash to the floor.

They thought that Mrs Turner had gone out to buy groceries, and were stunned when she knocked on the door, dividing the kitchen from the dining room.

"Come in," said Earnshaw as he blushed to the

roots of his hair, aware that she had heard his indulgences. Sally was undeterred and smiled brazenly at the servant.

"Oh, sir?" ventured Mrs Turner.

"Yes, Mrs Turner. What can I do for you on this freezing morning, eh?"

"I was wondering if I could have a word with you in private, sir?"

"Certainly. Is that all right with you, Sally?"

"I don't mind. I'll go upstairs to sleep off our fantastic energy expenditure."

"Please, Sally, there's no need for ribaldry. Go on up, there's a good girl."

"Sit down, would you, Mrs Turner," said Earnshaw. "You look terrified. What's the matter?"

"There's a funny-looking man outside. He stands at the top of the lane for hours on end. He's been there for several days, now. He's got a camera round his neck."

"Don't worry about him. He's probably a newspaper photographer. There's quite a famous actress living near here, isn't there? That must be the explanation."

"No, sir. There are no famous people living near here. He's no newspaper man. He's someone else. Just be careful, sir. That's my advice to you."

"What does he look like, the man?"

"Long, dark, dirty hair. Centre parting.

About 5'8" tall. Wears a filthy green and white sheepskin overcoat."

Earnshaw lit a cigar and after taking two puffs, he filled the room with smoke.

"This cigar bothering you, Mrs Turner?"

"No, sir."

"To get back to this man. Is he holding anything, or does he just have a camera round his neck?"

"Holding anything, sir?"

"I was just wondering what he does with his hands."

"He keeps them in his pockets."

"When you walk past him, does he give the impression that he might be carrying a gun?"

"No, sir. I don't think so."

"Then he couldn't be up to much. Does he ever speak to you?"

"Never. Not a word."

"Do you ever speak to him, if only to pass a remark about the weather?"

"I always say something about the weather when I walk past him. He doesn't answer. Yesterday, I asked him why he was standing in the lane. I told him it was private property. I threatened to call the police if he went on standing there. I said he'd be charged with suspicious loitering. He still didn't speak. He just gave me a peculiar smile."

"All right, Mrs Turner, I'll look into this, as this man is clearly upsetting you, when you're going about your lawful business. He sounds harmless. He's probably either plain rude or absolutely half-witted."

"He's no half-wit, sir. Neither am I. Someone's sent him here. It's something to do with you and the young lady."

"I see. Anything else worrying you, Mrs Turner?"

"Yes, sir, there is. This time it's something personal, something I feel I can talk to you about, as I served under your parents, God rest their souls."

"All right, Mrs Turner. Do get on with it."

"I was here, before you was born, sir, and I remember holding you when you was an innocent babe in arms. Begging your pardon, and with the greatest respect for you, sir, I had no idea that the baby boy I used to hold, would grow into a man with such disgusting, depraved, sexual habits."

"I beg your pardon, Mrs Turner?"

"Yes. Sexual habits, sir. And what about that lovely Meissen teapot you kicked off the table after breakfast?"

"Well, what about it?" asked Earnshaw, blushing.

"Your parents treasured that teapot and your

mother wouldn't even let me touch it. She washed it and dried it herself, and if she knew the way you smashed it to pieces, she'd turn in her grave, God bless her!"

"Come, now, Mrs Turner. You really are being dashed impertinent," said Earnshaw. "Anything else you wish to discuss?"

Mrs Turner was close to tears.

"It's not my business, but I feel such loyalty towards the house and the family I've served since I was little more than a girl, that I must say this, and I'll only say it the once."

"Oh, what will you say?"

"I do so wish you would marry the young lady, instead of living with her in sin. Begging your pardon, sir, you'd wash the honour of this house clean, if you did."

"But I can't, Mrs Turner. Don't you understand? I'd give anything to marry her but her husband won't give her a divorce." He put his arms round the servant, fearing that she might hand in her notice.

"She's already married? Now, I understand, sir. That man in the lane has been sent by an agent of her husband. The camera round his neck is to photograph you and your lady-friend, to give her husband the evidence he needs to divorce her. Once the picture is taken and things are sorted, you'll be free to marry."

"That may be what it looks like to you," said Earnshaw. "It's not the case. Sally's husband has told her he's going to kill me or have me killed, and it's not an empty threat. He's serious. He needs my photograph so that either he or my killer can identify me. I'm not scared, though. I've got a gun, too, and with my training in the Army, I know how to use it.

"I'm not a coward. I'm not afraid to leave this house. I loathe vindictiveness in others, and I'm not going to let anyone come between me and my happiness. I'm calling the police and, because I've served my country, I will be given special protection."

"Oh, Lord save us, sir!" murmured Mrs Turner. "I'm going home to make myself some hot, sweet tea and pray that there will be no bloodshed anywhere near this peaceful, happy house!"

Sally came into the room after Mrs Turner had left.

"I overheard it all, Ben," she said, "so there's no need to go over it again. I'm calling the police and I'm telling them about my husband's threat to murder you."

Earnshaw pinned her to the wall.

"I only told Mrs Turner I was calling the police, to placate her, to stop her getting scared and threatening to leave. Neither you nor I are calling them. I wore a uniform in the service of my country once, and I'm not running to a bunch of idle layabouts, just because they, too, wear uniforms. I'm not a coward, Sally. I don't ask people to protect me. A soldier fights his own battles.

"We'll pack two trunks to last us. Then we'll put them in the back of the Jag. We'll cover our faces with scarves so that, if this boy is out there, waiting to take my picture, he won't be able to."

Earnshaw carried the first of the two trunks to the car, his face covered and his eyes shielded by dark glasses. He went back in to collect the second trunk, and once that, too, was in the car, Sally came out and got into the passenger seat. Although it was not she whose life was at risk, she took the precaution of covering her face and hair as well, because Earnshaw had told her to.

Earnshaw engaged gear. He found it difficult to climb over the ice on the first and steepest part of the lane. There were another fifty yards to go along the flat before reaching the top.

"The bastard's still there," said Earnshaw. "Look how motionless he is. He might just as well be a statue."

Sally saw the man raise his head. He pulled his hands hurriedly out of his pockets and grabbed hold of his camera which he pointed at the car.

"He's no statue, Ben. Put your foot down and go straight at him. That way, he won't even be able to take your number," said Sally.

Earnshaw became excited again by Sally's commanding tone. He increased his speed to forty miles an hour. The man threw himself into the hedge to save his life.

James Buxton was frustrated by the prolonged inability of any of his snoopers to photograph Sally and Earnshaw.

He picked up his internal 'phone and rang through to a tiny basement room which the morning snooper, wearing the green and white sheepskin coat, came to to take instructions.

"Chris!" snapped Buxton.

"Yes, sir."

"I want you to come up to my office."

"I'm coming, sir."

"And another thing, I don't want to see you with that shabby overcoat still on your back. You will kindly hang it up in the corridor."

Chris did as he was told and sat in one of the chairs opposite Buxton's desk.

"You still haven't bothered to tidy yourself up, I see. Have you got a guitar?"

"No, sir."

"Get your bloody hair cut, then."

"Was there anything else, sir?"

"Was there anything else? Was there anything else? What the hell do you think? You were posted to Greenhill Lane to take photographs of Lt. Earnshaw and Mrs Bamber several days ago. I imagine he's got no idea of the fact that Mr Bamber wishes him tailed. I refuse to believe he hasn't left his house, if only to take a short stroll in the snow."

"Nor has he, sir."

"I don't believe that. I think you've been straying repeatedly from your post, to go to the pub, just to get out of the cold. Am I right?"

"No, sir," said Chris emphatically. "I was there all the bloody time..."

"Language, boy!"

"I'm sorry. I was there all the time, and near to freezing to death. Yesterday, about lunch-time, I saw a green Jag coming out of the garage next to Greenhill House. It raced up the lane and it was coming straight at me. I had to jump out of the way."

"Did you see the face or faces of anyone in it?"

"There were two people."

"A man and a woman?"

"I think so, but their faces were covered with scarves and dark glasses."

"That sounds like Earnshaw and his moll. If it had been a case of two others, they wouldn't have hidden their faces. So you couldn't get a photograph?"

"How could I, sir? Their whole faces were covered."

"Fair enough. Did you make a note of the number of the car?"

"I was able to do that. The number's UUU 688. It's a dark green Jaguar."

"What direction did it go in?"

"Through the woods, towards the town, sir."

"All right, Chris. Thank you for your efforts. You may go now, and don't forget to do something about your hair. It's a disgrace to the firm."

Buxton rang Bamber up in his London office.

"Call for you, Mr Bamber," said his personal assistant.

"Get his name, will you?"

"He won't give it, I'm afraid."

"All right, put him through."

"Mr Bamber?"

"Yes."

"James Buxton here. Are we able to talk?"

"No. Not here. Ring me at 10.00 tonight. I don't get home till then."

"10.00's a bit late."

"It's the only time I can talk."

"All right. I'll ring then."

"Have you any news?"

"Only a little. Not much. We can discuss that later."

Bamber was ten minutes late getting home. Another heavy fall of snow had delayed his train. Buxton rang at 10.30 between mouthfuls, while he and his wife were eating in the kitchen.

"I'm sorry, Mr Buxton. My train was late," said Bamber.

"No matter. The situation is this. Your wife left Greenhill House at lunch-time today in a green Jaguar, accompanied by Lt. Earnshaw."

"Did your man get a picture?"

"No. Their faces were covered with scarves and glasses."

"How do you know it was them?"

"That's obvious. They were hiding their faces. Also, they were seen coming out of the house one by one. Our man got the number of the car. It's UUU 688. Very regrettably, we've lost them for the time being, but we've got the number to go by."

"Where do you think they went?"

"I've no idea. I assume they've left the town for a while. That's what they'd do if they had any sense. Don't give up hope, though. They'll come back when they think the heat is off. Do you still want them tailed? If you do, it will be difficult and very costly."

"Leave it a few weeks," said Bamber. "I'll get back to you. I don't see the point of chasing them if we've no idea where they've gone."

Buxton picked up a pea which had rolled onto the floor from the spoon his wife was serving him with. He put it by the side of his plate.

"Quite so, Mr Bamber," he said. "We're sure to find them sooner or later. Give me a ring when you want me to re-open the case."

Sally and Earnshaw drove to the nearest port and boarded the ferry bound for France. Sally was aware of Earnshaw's costly private education and had come to regret her lack of cultural knowledge. She was self-conscious because her once prided executive secretary's skills, were devoid of any other field of learning.

She asked Earnshaw to drive her through Western Europe and to teach her the intricacies of architecture, show her the contents of art galleries, and familiarize her with the culture, customs and history of the countries they visited. This, he was able to do with a style which impressed her, and increased her love and admiration for him as a scholar, rather than merely a good-looking sex aid.

"How do you *know* all these things?" she asked him, while they were dining at a sophisticated *rive droite* restaurant in Paris.

"My parents used to take me round Europe during my school holidays," he said. "My mother was an unusually well-educated woman, and thrust so much culture down my throat that it became part of me, whether I wanted it that way, or not."

"Are you pleased she forced it on you?"

"I wasn't at the time, but I'm grateful to her, now. She made me read all the classics as well. She forced me to learn the dates of the kings and queens of England. She made me memorize passages from Shakespeare, as well as demanding that I learn the poems of Keats, Wordsworth, Shelley and others, by heart. She was a bit of a bully and sometimes she made me go without food, until I'd memorized the things she wanted me to."

"Surely that would have put you off scholarship for life?" said Sally, as she tried to extract her snail from its slippery shell.

"It did until I was about fifteen. Then, I realized that my knowledge was greater than that of my contemporaries. I started to feel superior to them, and I made sure that I was better than they at athletics, as well. By the age of eighteen, I was so proud of myself that I was convinced I could do anything they could not. I started chasing women, and even in that respect, I knew I was more accomplished than other young men of my age."

"Wouldn't you say that was being a bit arrogant?"

"Arrogant? No. Just a case of being self-confident. You have to be self-confident to survive, but luckily, I'm humble in the way I deal with others. I hope I've never shown any arrogance towards you."

"No, Ben. When I first met you, I had no idea you were so extraordinarily well-educated."

"That's because I hid it. That's why I may be a bit crude in some ways. When we first met, I didn't want to show off to you, for fear of talking down to you, and making you feel inferior."

"How did you feel about me at the beginning?"

"I was in love with you from the start."

"Why? You didn't know me."

"Because of the way you asked all those questions in that cinema. No-one else does that. Only you. That makes you unique. I wanted you then, just as I want you, now. I want you to leave that bastard and marry me. Even if he won't divorce you, I want us to live together until one of us is dead."

Sally wanted the same but found any mention of her husband too unpleasant to discuss. To show that she reciprocated Earnshaw's feelings, she kissed him lightly on the cheek.

"Do you still know the dates of all the kings and

queens of England?" she asked.

"Yes. From William the Conqueror to now."

"There are so many, I just don't believe you. Go on, recite them, all of them. Prove to me you can do it."

Earnshaw lowered his head in the same way as he did when reciting to his mother. Sally stared at him challengingly and disbelievingly. His eyes rolled back like those of a dog about to be whipped, and his voice took on a hypnotized, liturgic tone.

"William the First, 1066–1087
William the Second, 1087–1100
Henry the First, 1100–1135
Stephen, 1135–1154
Henry the Second, 1154–1189..."

Sally felt she had walked into something she couldn't get out of, as if she were sinking into a moorland bog. She had asked Earnshaw to continue until the present Queen, so she felt obliged to wait until the end.

He was now in a trance, unaware of his surroundings, and looked as if he were both yearning for chastisement and afraid of it at the same time. She sensed misery in his state, but her predominant emotions were those of irritation and boredom.

By the time he had reached Elizabeth the First, she was on the verge of losing her temper as he was reminding her of Bamber. She rapped him on the knuckles with her bread knife, and because she was drunk, she started shouting,

"All right, all right! There's no need to go through the whole bloody lot!"

He snapped out of the trance, suddenly realizing that the excitable woman with him was not his mother.

"Oh, sorry. I was asked to do them all," he said in a subservient tone.

"No matter. I want to hear more about the visits you made to Europe with your parents. While your mother was drumming culture into you, what was your father doing?"

"He wasn't interested. He wasn't a cultured man. He just used to wander off."

"Where did he go?"

"Up the disorderlies."

"What do you mean, up the disorderlies?"

"I meant he went to the disorderly houses."

"Do you mean the brothels?"

"Yes. The brothels."

"Well, say so, for God's sake!"

"You're not angry, are you?"

"No. I'm just amused."

"By what?"

"The funny words you use."

"You're not bored with me like you were with Bamber?"

"If I didn't find you anything other than lovable, vulnerable and exciting, I wouldn't be with you, would I?"

The fugitives drove through France. When they could take no more of the rich food, they visited Holland, Germany, Italy and Spain. By the time they considered it safe to return to England, the winter they had left behind, had turned into a hot, oppressive summer.

They had reached the outskirts of Farnham.

"Are you pleased we're going back to Greenhill House?" asked Earnshaw.

"We can't afford to go there, even now. That man's going to find us. I know him. You don't. He never gives up."

"I'm not going on the run for the rest of my life like an escaped convict. He's not driving me away from my own home. He hasn't even served his bloody country," stated Earnshaw assertively.

Sally began to cry.

"All right. Of course I want to go home, but I don't feel up to it, quite yet. Do you know of a hotel we can go to, until I feel more secure?"

"I can refuse a lady nothing," said Earnshaw.

"The Hogg's Back is the best hotel I know. It's in Farnham. That's the last place Bamber and his agents will expect to find us in. We'll stay there till you feel safe."

"Why wouldn't they find us in Farnham?"

"Come on, Sally. I've been trying to educate you all winter. Have you never read Edgar Allan Poe's story *The Purloined Letter*?"

"No."

"I won't waste time telling you. I know The Hogg's Back well. There's a New Year's Eve Party there, every year. I used to go as a boy. You'll laugh at this. There was this ghastly twelve-year-old boy called Craddock. God, he was an exhibitionist!

"Whenever, the National Anthem was being played, he used to scramble on top of the grand piano, using the keyboard the pianist was playing on, as some sort of stepping stone. Once he was on the piano, he pulled out one of those horrible piping instruments called a recorder. He waited until the National Anthem was over. Then he always played the same boring, bloody tune, *London Bridge is Falling Down.*"

"Didn't he play any other tune?"

"Some of us should be so lucky!"

"What can I do for you, sir and madam?" asked the middle-aged concierge at The Hogg's Back.

"We want a quiet room on the top floor of the hotel where we won't be disturbed. My wife's pregnant. Our house is being redecorated, so we want to stay for a few weeks and will pay you in cash, now."

"Well, that's excellent. What name is it?"

"Craddock," said Earnshaw. "Mr and Mrs Cyril Craddock."

"And your home address?"

"Greenhill House, Greenhill Lane, Farnham. May we use your carpark during our stay?"

"Yes, of course. Anyone staying in the hotel has the right to use the carpark. You both look tired after your journey. Shall I send some tea up to your room? It will be room 309 by the way, or if you wish, you can have 307 or 308. Room 309 is bigger and more comfortable. All those rooms have bathrooms, except there are no baths, only showers."

"We'll have room 309," said Earnshaw.

"And what about the tea?"

"We'd like that as well."

"Anything to go with it?"

Earnshaw turned to Sally.

"I don't want anything. Do you?"

"I'd like some toast and honey, please."

"That, you shall have. I'll get the porter to carry up your trunks. I see he'll have to make two journeys."

"Oh, just one thing," said Earnshaw.

"Yes, sir?"

"My wife is feeling so poorly, we won't be leaving our bedroom during our stay. We will want all meals in the room and are only prepared to come out when the room is being cleaned."

The concierge looked baffled. Sally and Earnshaw were inwardly worried because they feared he would find them odd and ask them to leave.

"Since you are paying in cash, and in advance, I see no problem," he said. "All the rooms have telephones, so you can 'phone for a doctor if anything's wrong. I can give you the names and numbers of two good local doctors."

"There won't be anything wrong. My wife is only three months' pregnant."

The room they were shown to was moderate in size, and rather than having a window to make it pleasant and airy, it had a skylight, which let in just enough natural light to make the prison-like surroundings bearable.

"God, Sally, how long have we got to stay in this one?" said Earnshaw.

"Only a few weeks. Although I said my husband would go on chasing us forever, even he will give up sooner or later."

"I don't really mind it, Sally. Army accommodation was worse than this. We've got each other, haven't we? Why don't you take off your clothes?"

She did so. They did the same thing repeatedly every day for the following few weeks. Earnshaw read to Sally, from time to time. They were depressed at first but after a week, they adapted to the routine that Bamber had forced on them.

They had stayed in the room for two weeks. The friendly cleaner, the only person they had contact with, told them there would be an old-aged pensioners' function that evening.

"That sounds rivetting," said Sally, as she sat at the dressing table, smothering her face with thick make-up, having put on mascara-soaked false eyelashes a quarter of an inch thick. She had always worn crudely applied make-up, and because it excited Earnshaw, she wore twice as much as before, which made her look like a prostitute.

"I should imagine so," Earnshaw said. "Although it doesn't sound very stimulating, we've been incarcerated in here for so long, that I'd be prepared to get out, if only to see a whole lot of trolley-loads of stiffs. Damn it, Sally, some elderly people can be quite interesting to talk to."

"What if anyone sees us and tells my husband?"

"Don't be ridiculous. He doesn't mix with

people like that. He never sees anyone. Once he comes back from London, he goes straight to bed."

"Do you really want to go?"

"Yes," said Earnshaw assertively. "I've had enough of this room."

"All right, Ben. You're always so good to me. Of course, we'll go."

At least fifty pensioners, many of them drunk, got out of a coach and went into the hotel at 8.00 p.m. The only two visitors who didn't use the coach, arrived in a second-hand, battered Triumph which they left in the carpark.

A man opened the heavily dented driver's door with considerable difficulty. He was in his early twenties, light in stature and had short, well-combed black hair, parted in the centre. He was wearing a poorly-fitting tuxedo which he had hired for the evening.

He walked round to the passenger's side and opened the door, which, like the driver's door, was covered with scratches and dents. He leant into the car and handed the walking-stick on the floor to a frail old lady who gripped it in her severely arthritic right hand.

"Ready to get out, Ma?" said the man.

"Yes. I'm all right, dear. Just hold my arm, will you."

It took the man a few minutes to help his

disabled, prematurely aged mother out of the car. She leant against it, smoothing down her white hair, while her son's eyes wandered with envy to two other parked cars nearby. One was a brand new Rolls Royce. The other was a green Jaguar, covered with at least half an inch of dust. The mother, who knew her son almost as well as he knew himself, realized that he had been reminded of something he might otherwise have forgotten.

He took a handkerchief from his pocket and wiped the number plate. He saw the number UUU 688 and jumped backwards, smiling.

"What in the world are you doing, Chris?" said his mother. "What do you want with that car? My feet are hurting. Help me into the hotel."

"That car's been here for weeks on end, judging by the dust on it. It must belong to someone who's been staying in the hotel all that time," he said, smiling.

"So what?" said his mother angrily. Her feet were getting even more painful. "Of what conceivable interest is that to me? Besides, I want to go to the bathroom. I thought I understood you but I don't think I do. What on earth are you smiling at?"

"Nothing. Just in a good mood."

His mother banged the ground with her walking-stick. She resented it whenever her son smiled or laughed in front of her without sharing the joke.

"I may be old and stupid, but at least I can appreciate what is decent!" she said.

"Oh, I'm sorry. I didn't mean to be rude."

"All right, then. I will credit you with one thing. At least that boss of yours, whoever he is, has forced you to keep your hair nice and short and tidy. You used to look like a right, regular little beatnik. I was embarrassed to be seen in public with you, and when anyone asked me who you were, I told them you were a workman to whom I was showing the way."

He was mildly irritated by his mother's tetchiness, particularly as his boss was permanently criticizing him, despite his anxiousness to please him. He had had a long, unproductive day, trying to find the kidnapper of a twelve-year-old boy, and was too tired to enter into an argument with his mother.

"Come on. Let's go in, Ma. I know your dress will look prettier than all the other ladies' dresses," he forced himself to remark.

He escorted his mother to the large dining room where other pensioners were standing, drinking sherry. He noticed a young couple at the end of the room, and observed Sally's escort's extreme good looks, in comparison with his sallow, seedy facial features.

"Sherry, Ma?"

"Not just now. I've got to go to the bathroom."

"Will you be all right finding it on your own, or would you like me to ask one of the waitresses to help you?"

"Look here, boy! I'm not that old, although I may look it. I'm capable of putting one foot in front of another. I'm not dead yet!" she shouted.

A few pensioners, topping up their already intoxicated states with sherry, turned round and giggled at the mother and son. Chris said,

"Please don't speak to me like that. It's awfully humiliating, particularly as I was only trying to make things easier for you."

"Oh, we *are* misunderstood, aren't we? You know I don't really mean it. I'll see you in about ten minutes. Get yourself some sherry."

Chris walked towards the young man and woman at the end of the room, with a glass of orange juice in his hand. He would have preferred sherry to ease his permanent tension, both at work, and at home. He hid behind an exceptionally inebriated old gentleman, who stood on his own, trying to dance the Charleston.

Sally's appearance was identical to the description Buxton had given Chris on Bamber's instructions. He looked closely at Earnshaw and memorized his attractive features, so that he knew whose photograph he had to take at another time. He allowed for the possibility that Sally might leave him for another man, just as she had left Bamber.

Neither Sally nor Earnshaw noticed him, and even if he had stood in front of them, they would not have recognized him after the change in his appearance.

Like the pensioners, they too had drunk themselves senseless, and threw themselves into an uninhibited, passionate embrace. Chris no longer needed to look at them as he had a photographic visual memory. Apart from that, their faces were now crushed against each other and their features obscured.

He felt someone tapping him on the shoulder.

"Oh, Ma?"

"I've had some sherry. It's pretty strong. Not bad here, is it?"

"It's all right. Did you have any trouble finding your way?"

"Not really. I do wish you'd stop gaping at that couple over there. You've taken a shine to that brazen, blonde hussy, haven't you? You didn't know I was watching you, but I saw the way you were ogling her. A married woman, too, I shouldn't wonder. It's time you found a girl of your own, instead of boring your eyes through an attached woman's head, like a couple of burning screwdrivers."

"I wasn't staring at her, Ma. I was just standing, thinking?"

"Thinking? Thinking? A thought has never passed through your head in your life, has it, you little simpleton?"

"Oh, please, Ma, do stop it. I've got to go out now, too. Sit down over here. When I come back, please try to be nice to me for a change. My boss asked me to do overtime tonight. I said I couldn't, just so that I could bring you here to enjoy yourself."

Chris went straight into the hotel lobby, where some more pensioners had gathered, after taking their drinks out of the crowded dining room.

A woman, aged about fifty, was leaning over the desk, talking to the middle-aged concierge, with whom Sally and Earnshaw had registered. The other concierge, a much younger man, who had never met them, had been told to man the desk that evening, but he had rung up at the last minute to say he was ill.

Chris stood near the middle-aged woman, a cleaner working overtime, and waited for her to finish her conversation with the concierge, so that he could speak to her. This was unnecessary, however, as he overheard their conversation and found out what he wished to know.

"This is the first time I've seen that couple outside their room on the top floor," said the cleaner.

The concierge was thinking about something else.

"What couple?" he asked, absentmindedly.

"Those people who checked in fairly recently. The young blonde woman and that dish of a man. I always thought there was something odd about them.

"Whenever I come to do their room, they stand in the corridor, facing the wall, so close to it, their heads nearly touch it. I don't call myself clever, and never did, but I know they're running away from something. I wonder if it's the Law."

"Oh, that couple," said the concierge. "It's true they haven't left their room until now, but it's not my business to bother them as they paid in cash for the weeks they wished to stay. I gave them room 309, didn't I?"

"Yes, that's right. Definitely 309. I'm not that bright, but one thing I never forget is a number. Mind you, I don't know how they can bear being up there for so long. There are no windows. Just a skylight. There are skylights in all the rooms on the top floor. Always have been."

The concierge believed in minding his own business. He was not interested in anyone but himself. He appeared bored, but didn't want to seem rude to the cleaner.

"That's right," he said, forcing himself to smile. "There have always been skylights up there — ever since this place was built."

"And there's another thing," said the cleaner, whose tongue had been loosened by the four glasses of sherry she had surreptitiously consumed. "I've overheard this couple a few times. Well, to tell you the truth, I've been so intrigued, I've often listened through the door. I've heard the man say things like, 'I'm not spending the rest of my life in hiding. I'm no coward. I'm not afraid of anyone. I've served my country. That man hasn't.'

"I've heard the woman say things like, 'We've got to stay here a bit longer before it's safe.' I also heard her say, 'He's made up his mind to kill you and he'll never give up. He's a vicious, jealous husband. If he doesn't kill you himself, he'll have you followed so that he can get someone else to do it.'"

The concierge's former boredom diminished.

"You heard all that? Are you sure?"

"Yes, but don't get the wrong impression. If I spend the odd five minutes eavesdropping, I always make up the time afterwards to earn my keep."

"Oh, yes, I'm sure you do. About this couple, they asked me if they could leave their car in the carpark all this time. I know it's the summer, but the battery must be flat by now. I've been out to see it. It's covered in dust and it looks fit for the scrapyard. It must have been a lovely car, once. Green Jaguars are so elegant when they're clean and polished."

The cleaner was aware that she was rather drunk, and she eased her weight back from the desk, to prevent the concierge smelling alcohol on her breath.

"I know that car. I had no idea it belonged to that weird couple," she said. "I thought it had been dumped. I thought they was waiting for it to be collected for re-cycling."

"Oh, it's not quite as bad as that," said the concierge. "Hold on. I'll look up the people in 309 and I'll find its number, just to confirm whether it really is their car."

The cleaner was feeling even more intoxicated. It took her longer than it took others, for alcohol to hit her brain.

"Aw, go on! There's nothing I love more than being an amateur detective. I shouldn't be a cleaner, should I, eh?"

The concierge flicked through the register. "Ah, yes. The couple in 309 own a British racing green Jaguar, registration number UUU 688. I know its colour because I was in the carpark the day after they'd registered. I linked the colour with the number because it's such an easy number to remember.

"When they arrived, they registered under the names of Mr and Mrs Cyril Craddock, of Greenhill House, Greenhill Lane, Farnham. If what you've told me is true, it's obvious that's a false name. No-one in hiding gives their real name. Most of our customers automatically produce identification, such as a driving licence or a passport, and they almost always do so without being asked.

"This couple didn't, but, frankly, I really don't care. I've taken their money. They're quiet. They never make a nuisance of themselves, so whether they're hiding, or indeed who they're hiding from, is of absolutely no interest to me."

"May I come up to your office to see you, Mr Buxton?" The time was 9.05 the following morning.

"You may, Chris. My next appointment is not until 10.00. What's it to do with? Are you handing in your notice, or do you want a rise?"

"Neither, sir. I've got more information about the Bamber case."

"You have. Come on up, straight away."

Chris did not feel ill at ease in Buxton's office this time, as he knew his boss would be pleased with him.

"Well, Chris?"

"Last night, I took my elderly mother to a pensioners' party at The Hogg's Back Hotel."

"Very interesting. Either get to the point or shut up."

"I found Lt. Earnshaw's Jaguar, registration number UUU 688 in the hotel carpark. It was covered in dust. This led me to believe that Earnshaw and Bamber's wife were, not only staying in the hotel, but had been there for some time."

"What makes you think that? Earnshaw may have dumped the car there and gone off somewhere else."

"That's not so. When I went into the dining room where the pensioners were drinking, I saw a youngish man and woman sitting alone at the end of the room. I studied them from a distance. The woman matched the description Mr Bamber gave you, a hundred per cent."

"How were the two of them behaving?"

"Like a couple who were crazy about each other."

"What did the man look like?"

"Dark brown hair, moustachiod, well built. Thirty-ish. Overpoweringly handsome. Radiated concentrated sex from every part of him."

"Are you a queer?" asked Buxton aggressively.

"Certainly not, sir! But I can always tell what a

woman sees in a man."

"No man on earth can tell what a woman finds attractive in another man," said Buxton. "Continue."

"I went to the hotel lobby. It was pretty crowded so no-one noticed me. I listened to a conversation at the concierge's desk. It was a frank, friendly conversation between the concierge and a cleaner, very much the worse for wear, doing overtime that night. The cleaner said the couple occupied a room on the top floor, with a skylight.

"She said they had been there for some weeks and until last night, had refused to leave their room. She also said she had been so intrigued by the way they refused to leave their room, that she often listened to their private conversations. She said the man resented being in hiding for the rest of his life. The woman said she was afraid to leave the hotel because her jealous, vicious husband wished to kill him."

"Kill him?" exclaimed Buxton.

"That's what the cleaner heard her say."

"Maybe that's just hysteria on her part. Mr Bamber expressed no intention whatever of killing his wife's lover. Go on."

"The concierge also said that this couple gave their address as Greenhill House, Greenhill Lane, Farnham and, if it's of any use to you, sir, he said their room number was 309 on the top floor."

Buxton looked briefly through the Bamber file and made a note of some of the matching evidence, namely the description of Sally, the Jaguar's registration number, as seen leaving the house, and again in the hotel carpark, and most significant of all, Earnshaw's address, not only given by Bamber, but also entered in the hotel register.

There was a pause, while Buxton continued to write notes. The younger man yearned for praise from his employer, if only once during his service.

"Very well done, Chris!" said Buxton, adding, "There's just one more thing that has to be done before the Bamber case is over."

"Sir?"

"I want you to cover the hotel, until you get a picture of them both."

"I'll do that, sir."

"Did either of them see you?"

"No. I hid behind an elderly drunk."

"Are you quite sure you weren't seen?"

"Quite sure, sir."

"Since you've been on this case, has anyone else connected with Earnshaw, seen you?"

"Yes. In January, a woman buying things for him walked past me regularly, when you posted me in Greenhill Lane."

"Did she speak to you?"

"Yes. She never stopped passing remarks about the weather."

"Did you speak to her at all?"

"No."

"Not even when she tried to make friendly conversation?"

"Not even then."

"Still, she must have mentioned you to Earnshaw and described your appearance. Also, they would have both seen you standing there, when they drove off."

"My hair looks different, now that it's shorter. Also, when they drove past me, they only saw me fleetingly."

"Yes. I do see that," said Buxton. "The firm will pay for you to register yourself in the hotel. Now that the pair have had the courage to leave their room once, they will get bolder and do so again."

Chris registered under his own name. He had all his meals in the dining room, and spent each day in the lounge, the only part of the hotel where there was a television. He also befriended the senior concierge by finding out what few interests he had outside his work, and being generally pleasant and affable.

"We've got yet another function this Saturday," the concierge said after Chris had been in the hotel for three days. "These functions bring in most of our income, as we don't get many customers here, like we did in the old days."

"What sort of a function is it?" asked Chris.

"It's the Mayor of Guildford's sixtieth birthday. It's a stand-up affair. I suppose what few residents there are in the hotel, will look in on it, at least some of them, at any rate."

"Is he very well liked, the Mayor?"

"I've never met him. I've heard he's not a bit what you'd imagine a mayor to be. It's been said that he takes his duties seriously and responsibly, but once he's off duty, he loses all his inhibitions, and is prone to loud behaviour, and has a penchant for the bottle.

Apparently, his wife is not only very musical, but actually writes music."

"What sort of music?" asked Chris, whose only interest was in getting a pay rise from Buxton.

"Jazz, or so I've heard."

Chris disliked Jazz. He found the concierge dull, and was now struggling to make conversation.

"I played the saxophone once," he said after a pause. "I've lost my touch now, I'm afraid."

"Well, do come along, sir. You may make a few friends."

Until Saturday, Sally and Earnshaw remained in

their room. It was the indiscreet cleaner who mentioned the function to them.

"We are going to be there," said Earnshaw firmly, once the room had been cleaned.

"I'm not so scared this time," said Sally. "I feel safer now. We've survived one gathering and nothing happened. My odious husband doesn't like Jazz, and I don't think anyone he associates with, likes it either. I personally adore it. What is more, I've got a feeling the heat may be off. I want to get out of here and go home."

The dining room on the Mayor's sixtieth birthday was more crammed with heaving, sweating bodies, than the London underground at rush hour. The Mayor's wife played loud piano music, which Earnshaw couldn't stand, but which pleased him because of the relaxing effect it had on Sally.

Chris circulated round the room, taking photographs of the Mayor, his frumpish wife thumping the keyboard, and other people selected at random.

Sally and Earnshaw collected repulsive food from the buffet. They had no choice but to sit near the Mayor's table, because the other tables were full. They both drank considerable quantities of poor quality, lukewarm, white wine, and as they were unable to eat the food, they sat holding each other and giggling.

Chris continued to circulate. The Mayor, was also inebriated. He shovelled spoonfuls of birthday cake, saturated with whipped cream, into his mouth.

"Another picture of you please, if I may, with your kind permission, Your Worship," shouted Chris, straining his vocal cords above the earsplitting piano playing.

"Why, of course. And who might you be?" shouted the Mayor, his mouth crammed with cake and cream, covering his chin.

"Mick Gracey, sir. *Farnham News.*"

"*Farnham News*? I don't think I've heard of that newspaper. Never mind. Take a picture all the same."

Chris took pictures of the Mayor's closest associates, sitting at his table. He changed the film with the speed of a professional newspaper cameraman. He moved to the next table, where Sally and Earnshaw, now too drunk to know where they were, sat caressing each other.

"Smile, everybody, please. Look straight at the camera, ladies and gentlemen. That goes for the happy newly-weds, too."

Sally and Earnshaw were delirious with joy. They felt free. They were going home in a few days. Their blood was awash with wine, and their mutual adoration and euphoria had reached a peak so high, that they felt they had hit Mars.

"Go on, newsboy, take our pic!" said Sally. She turned to Earnshaw. "Shall I pull down my dress, just for a second?"

"Oh, yes! Go on, Sally, that's the stuff. Show the jolly old newsboy your big, buxom assets, what!" His excessive alcohol consumption had intensified his public school accent.

"Beautiful!" said Chris, as he clicked the camera on Sally's exposed chest. "And another, and a third for luck. While we're at it, I'll take your pretty profile as well." Sally wriggled about, throwing back her head and laughing, showing her upper and lower jaw to flaunt her white, even teeth.

"Thank you, ma'am, thank you. Now, it's the handsome gentleman's turn. Let's have a frontal and a profile, sir. Something you can show to your grand-children. Good. That's the way to do it. You're a natural, you are, sir, no doubt about it. And now, we'll have a few shots of you with your arms round the lovely lady. One final one. No need to be shy, now. Put your hand on her chest. Give her a fondle, to show how much you love her. Excellent! The day these pictures come out, will be the happiest day of your lives...."

"Mr Buxton?"

"Yes, Chris."

"I've now confirmed that the couple have been

living at The Hogg's Back Hotel for some weeks and are still living there. I've got the pictures. They'll knock you sideways, sir."

"I'll be the judge of that. Bring them up, straight away."

Buxton sifted through the pile of photographs. He blew out and made a loud whistling noise.

"Chris?"

"Sir?"

"Go over to the drinks cabinet, will you, and get me a stiff whisky and soda."

"Yes, sir. Anything else?"

"Yes. From now on, you'll be getting a pound an hour instead of ten shillings."

"Why, thank you, sir!"

Buxton rang Bamber in London.

The tycoon picked up the 'phone himself.

"Mr Bamber."

"Yes. Is that Mr Buxton?"

"It is. All the work you asked us to do has been completed. It has been confirmed that the pair have been hiding in The Hogg's Back Hotel in Farnham, and are continuing to stay there. They are in room 309 which has a skylight. It's on the top floor. The concierge has confirmed that the couple have left a green Jaguar in the hotel carpark. It has the same registration number as the car seen leaving Lt.

Earnshaw's house in January — UUU 688. The photographs you require are now on my hands. Would you like me to send them to your home address, or would you prefer to come to my office and collect them?"

"I'd rather you sent them to my home address. Don't send them in the post. Send them by taxi. Are they small enough to go through a letter-box?"

"No. The stiff envelope containing them will be too big for that."

"That will be all right. Mrs Blackstock, my housekeeper, will be there to open the door.

"Could you please get a detailed written report typed out as well?"

"No problem. I'll send it in the same envelope. The photographs are good, Mr Bamber. You will find them to your entire satisfaction, but I have to warn you, they are not very pleasant."

"I see. Do I owe you any more money?"

"Just a small sum to cover the hotel room our photographer had to occupy for a few days, in order to catch the two offending parties. You will receive the bill shortly. Be sure to contact us again if you require our services."

Bamber opened the envelope on his return at 10.00 that evening. It would be an understatement to say that he was homicidal. The emotion he felt was far worse than that. His rage was too enormous for him to smash all the crockery his mother had left him in her will. His blood pressure soared to such a dizzying height that he fainted.

The habits of Campbell, Bamber's Scottish travelling companion, were like clockwork. Once more, there were no seats on the train. Bamber found his friend the morning following his shock. He was leaning against the window in the same part of the corridor as always, singing to himself.

Bamber kept his hideous rage within and remained outwardly calm. The only sign that he had been traumatized, was manifested in his heavy breathing.

"Morning, Claude. You look as if you had to run for the train, today. Overslept, did you?"

Bamber was not accustomed to showing emotion, but he gripped Campbell by the arm, with tears in his eyes.

"Whatever's wrong? Are you in debt or something?"

"Oh, Bill, I've been too embarrassed to speak to you about this, before. It's about my wife."

"Sorry to hear that. Is she not well? Is it some ladies' disease? Tell me about it. You'll feel a wee bit better, I'm sure."

"No, it's not that. It's adultery. She's left me for her good-looking fancy fellow. I've set a private dick on them. His firm sent me an agonizing, detailed report of what's been going on between them. That's not the worst of it." Bamber continued to breathe heavily and made a retching noise.

"Come on, man. What is the worst of it?"

"The firm sent me a lot of photographs of them together. They were all over each other. It was sheer pornography. The man looks like some ravishing Hollywood rake. Oh, God! I'm so livid and so hurt, I just want to die, but I want to kill the swank, swaggering bastard, first."

"You want to kill him? Are you serious?".

"I'm in deadly earnest, Bill. I've got to kill him, or get someone else to do so. It's got to be done so that I don't have to spend the rest of my life in hell." Bamber started weeping and hugged the perplexed Scotsman. "It's my honour, Bill. Can't you see? My honour has been besmirched."

"Calm down, man!" said Campbell. "You're in luck. I can help you. You've been such a good friend to me that I'm going to help you."

"How, Bill?"

"Underworld contacts in London. I'll say no more. Bring me the detective's report and the photographs this time tomorrow."

"You know someone?"

"Yes. Someone who knows who can be approached."

"Who? Come on, out with it!"

"You heard me, didn't you, Claude? I can tell you nothing until you bring me the report and the pictures tomorrow. Then you'll tell me the whole story."

Campbell went to the London Hospital and had an extended lunch break. He took the underground train to a station nearest to an East End pub. He went straight to the bar.

"Joe?" he called, straining his voice above a high-pitched, whining Beatles song, blaring over a loudspeaker.

"'Ullo, Bill, I 'aven't seen you for months. Not very civil of you since we was children together."

"Let's go into the corner away from this bloody noise, so that we can talk. God, I hate the Beatles! Their voices are so effeminate. I bet they're as queer as nine bob notes."

"All, right, Bill. 'Ave a drink on me. What'll you have?"

"A pint of Carlsberg. Let's go. I haven't much time."

The two men sat in the corner. The music was less loud but they could only just hear each other.

"What's this in aid of, Bill?"

"Are you still in contact with the Family?"

"What family?"

"*The* family, of course. The Family whose name you refuse to give. The Family who do hit jobs."

"Ah! Now, you're talking. Yes. I still send people to them, as I get a small cut."

"I'm friends with this desperate tycoon. His wife's gone off with someone. He wants the man killed and I'm sure he'd be prepared to pay anything."

"Do you know any more?"

"No. My friend's bringing the private dick's written report and the photographs to me, tomorrow. I'd like to bring them to the Family then."

"OK, I'll mention this to the person running the Family. I'll contact that person straight away, just so as the whole lot of them can be prepared."

"Why so discreet, Joe? Who's this person?"

"No names, but a really tough, frightening woman runs it. Her three sons carry out her orders."

Kelvin and Alan Vernon had been giving their younger brother, Eddy, lessons in crime for several years, as well as taking him to deserted places for shooting lessons to prepare him for hitman jobs. He remained rather slow-witted, but was an unusually good shot and his mother, Olive, was impressed by Kelvin's reports of his skills.

It was during the hot summer of 1963. Alan and Eddy caught a throat virus, brought on by the hot weather. They were nursed at home by Olive, whose immune system was so impeccable that she had never had an illness in her life.

It was a Wednesday. Kelvin left the house for a drink, before the late lunch he was due to have alone with his mother. He often felt in awe of her, and needed a pint of beer before returning to the house and eating alone with her.

He was surprised to find the house devoid of the smell of cooking. He thought his mother had caught the virus as well, and was relieved by the assumption that he wouldn't have to eat with her, unaccompanied.

He heard the sound of the wireless in the living room. He was puzzled and went straight in. A hymn-singing programme was being broadcast which was unusual for a Wednesday, and the hymn, *From Greenland's Icy Mountains*, was being played with the volume turned up loudly.

Olive was sitting in her customary chair, with her shoes on the floor and her stockinged feet on her quilted stool. Her hands rested by her sides and her head was thrown back. Her dark hair was no longer plaited on top of her head, but was hanging loose, reaching her waist. Kelvin looked at her more closely, and noticed that her face was awash with tears and her whole body was shaking.

"What is it, Mother? Have you caught it, too?" he asked.

"No, boy! I've caught nothing. Please be quiet."

"What's the matter?"

"Listen to this hymn, boy."

"I didn't know you were devout."

"Nor may I be. It's the most beautiful and wonderful thing I have ever heard. Just listen to it."

"Yes, it's nice, isn't it?"

Olive turned the volume even higher.

"It's more than nice. I could listen to it for twenty-four hours a day for the rest of my life and never tire of it. Should I die before you, I want you to see to it that it's played at my funeral."

"Don't be a berk, Mother. You're not going to die."

"Not yet, I'm not, but will you see to it that this one wish of mine is granted? I know I shall hear it when the time comes, becoffined and beshrouded though I may be. I shall hear every single note."

Kelvin looked baffled.

"All right, Mother. I won't let you down," he said, "and I'll tell Alan and Eddy, too, just in case I go first."

The hymn came to an end. Olive turned the wireless off.

"There's something else I need to tell you."

"What, Mother?"

"There's a chance we may have a big contract on the way. I've just had a 'phone call from that Joe. Always so helpful he is."

"What sort of contract?"

"Nothing's definite, but it's possible someone's going to want his wife's lover done. The man's a tycoon, Joe's friend said, and he might be prepared to part with a fortune. If this works, we'll be able to leave this cold, damp country, and live somewhere sunny, where money grows on trees, like California."

"When's Joe sending the tycoon's friend to us, Mother?"

"Tomorrow. They were drinking together when I got the call. You were out. I told Joe he could send his friend straight to The Sawdust pub."

"What time, tomorrow?"

"Mid-day."

"If the tycoon tells his friend he's serious, who's going to do his wife's lover in?"

Olive laughed like a raucous old street woman.

"We'll give it to Eddy, stupid. He's one of the best shots you could find, and brains are not important."

Kelvin said, "I know Eddy never comes to our meetings, but surely he'll have to come this time, if he's the one who's doing a major job like this. I'm sure Alan will agree."

"Yes. There's no doubt about that. The boy's got to come this time," said Olive.

Bamber and Campbell met once more in the corridor of the train the following morning. Campbell said,

"I saw my friend in London. He's told me where I can find the people who will kill your wife's lover. It's a family. They're professionals. I'm seeing them at lunch-time today. Have you got the detective's report and the photographs with you?"

"Yes." Bamber's shaking hand pulled the stiff envelope from his briefcase. "It's all here. It's horrible. I want the bastard killed!"

"Keep your voice down."

They were interrupted by a pale-faced, bowler-hatted traveller, with a rolled up copy of *The Financial Times* under his arm, who was walking towards them from the other end of the corridor. Campbell grabbed Bamber by the arm.

"Get in the lavatory. Quick!"

Campbell threw open the vacant lavatory door. He seized Bamber by the shoulders and pushed him in in front of him, before kicking the door shut, and locking it. Bamber went white and started to hyperventilate.

Campbell had no medical knowledge, or even

rudimentary experience in first aid, and feared his companion might be having a heart attack. His legs were aching because he had been standing in the corridor almost every day, as well as having to push a heavy tea trolley round The London Hospital. He was therefore averse to the idea of running up and down the train, to ask if there were a doctor on board.

"Och, Claude, are you all right, mate?"

Bamber began to cry and threw his arms round the Scotsman, who wondered whether he would be able to handle a situation as emotionally taxing as this.

"Sit on the lavatory!" he commanded, and gave him a violent push. "I'll be OK standing up. Take deep breaths, and for Christ's sake calm down."

Bamber obeyed. "I'm all right now," he said, his voice still no more than a whisper.

"Hand over the envelope. Come on, man! We haven't got far to go before we get to London. Well done. That's better. Can I take all this stuff out."

"All right, Bill."

"This typed sheet, is it the report?"

"Yes."

"Can I read it."

"I *want* you to."

Campbell read it briefly. He had a retentive memory. He memorized the key words, Hogg's

Back Hotel. Room 309. Top floor. Skylight. Green Jaguar, registration number UUU 688.

"Oh, God, Bill! I want the filthy bastard killed. It's all in the report. That Lt. Earnshaw's a stinking, smug, ex-Army creep. To think they've been hiding in the Hogg's Back Hotel all this time, like a couple of animals. I'd be prepared to part with a thousand pounds to have him killed. I'd even be prepared to go up to two thousand," he cried, getting recklessly carried away by his pain.

"Lower your voice, man. You can be heard in the corridor. Can I see the pictures?"

"Yes. They're the worst of all. When I saw them last night, they very nearly killed me outright. I think, if I ever had to look at them again, I'd die."

"All right. There's no need for you to see them again, if you've already done so. Let's take a look."

Campbell held them close to the window to get a better view of them. He had to turn his back on Bamber, as he found them so sexually stimulating. He was yet another of the many men who were turned on by the sight of a common-looking, over-painted, peroxide blonde, with a large bust, being mauled by a man's hand. He wanted copies of all the photographs to cover his lavatory wall at home.

"I'll have to take copies of these," he said, still with his back to Bamber. "I'll need them to get them passed on to the killer of your wife's lover."

"But I shan't be wanting them back. I don't even want them near me."

"OK. No copies needed. I'll just hand the originals over, so that the killer will recognize the man when the time comes."

"Who's this man you saw yesterday?" asked Bamber.

"His name's Joe. He's been in crime all his life. He knows a family of professional killers, who meet to discuss operations in a semi-deserted East End pub, used, almost entirely, by themselves. The family consists of a mother, a terrifying harridan of a woman, and her three sons. She's in charge. She organizes contract killings, and gives the orders to whatever son she chooses to hit the target."

"Just who *are* all these people?"

"I can't give their names as I don't know them."

At exactly 12.00 the next day, Campbell came into the Sawdust pub.

Before him, sat the entire Vernon family, including Eddy. They were sitting on one side of a chipped oak table, facing the door. Apart from the barman, who was standing twenty yards away, drying glasses behind the bar, the pub was empty. Whenever word went round that the Vernons were using it for business, no-one, who feared damage to their person, went in there.

Campbell sat down opposite the Vernons, all of whom were chain-smoking. He took some tobacco from his pocket and rolled a cigarette.

"Eddy, go and get everyone half a pint of beer and no more," said Olive. Eddy obeyed. Once everyone had drained their glasses, the atmosphere became more relaxed.

"So Joe told you about me and my sons?" said Olive.

"Aye," said the Scotsman.

"We know Joe well. We also know him well enough to trust him not to give you our surname. And who are you?"

"My name's William Campbell."

"What do you want from us, Mr Campbell?"

"An old train friend wants his wife's lover sorted."

"What do you mean — a 'train friend?'" asked Olive in an intimidating tone.

"He's a very rich man. We're old friends. He and I travel on the same train to London every morning."

"What, to work?"

"Yes."

"If he's so rich, why does he need to work?"

"To get richer."

Olive smiled. "And you? Meaning no disrespect,

you look too old to work."

"I'm retired. I travel to London to do voluntary work in a hospital."

"Which hospital?"

Campbell lied, instinctively, for fear of being tailed.

"The Marsden."

"Why do you work when you aren't paid?"

"To stop myself going mad."

"In that case, perhaps you're mad, already. I'm only joking. How much can your friend part with?"

"He said a thousand pounds, but he's so angry and desperate, he'd be prepared to up it to two," said Campbell unwisely, for he was only a humble man, trying to help a suffering friend, and not an experienced business negotiator. He regretted his words.

"Our price is two, not one," said Olive.

"All right. He won't go higher than two. I'm sure of that."

"How do you know?"

"I know him just as I know myself. I know his boundaries."

"Does he know exactly where his wife and her lover are?"

"Yes. He hired a detective. They're living in the Hogg's Back Hotel in Farnham, Surrey. Room 309.

Top floor. Skylight. They keep a green Jaguar, registration number UUU 688 in the hotel carpark."

"Cheeky, eh? What's your friend's name?"

"Do I have to give it?"

"If he wants anything out of us, he'll have to let us know his name."

"OK. It's Claude Bamber," said Campbell after an uneasy pause, adding, "You never gave me your name, or the names of the young men sitting with you, although I know one of them's called Eddy, because I heard you address him."

"I'm not prepared to give my name," said Olive, "or the names of the men with me. It's just by chance that you know Eddy, but that's only his nickname. His real name is quite different. When are you next going to see Mr Bamber?"

"This evening. On the train leaving Waterloo Station."

"Good. You can tell him that my sons and I are not prepared to accept anything under two thousand pounds. Tell him to put the notes in a plastic bag and give the bag to you. Bring it to us tomorrow at mid-day, at the same place."

"Yes, I'm sure I can do that."

"Before you leave, tell us what your friend's wife looks like."

"A bit plump. Pretty. Looks like Diana Dors."

"Her name?"

"Sally Bamber."

"What's her lover's name?"

"Ben Earnshaw."

"What's he look like?"

"Just take a look at the photographs I've got here. I've also got the private dick's report with me."

Olive flicked through them and gave them to Eddy. "Right brazen hussy," she muttered.

Eddy looked lingeringly at each photograph in turn. There was an undisguised look of lechery in his eyes as he scrutinized Sally's exposed chest.

"You're supposed to study them, not ogle them, and you can take that smirk off your face! Look at the man, not the hussy. He's the one who's got to go. You really are a disgusting young man!" said Olive.

"It was the man I was looking at, Mother," said Eddy, defensively.

"Liar!" said Olive. She turned to Campbell who was struggling to keep a straight face. "Let's have the private dick's report, then, Mr Campbell. We'll study it and will find out all there is to know about your friend, Bamber, his tarty wife, Sally, and Ben Earnshaw."

"His full name is Lt. Kenneth Francis Benjamin Earnshaw," said Campbell. "That's all in the report."

"A Lieutenant, eh? Gone up in the world, has he? It's always the loosest women who go for Army men."

Campbell and Bamber met on the evening train from Waterloo station. Campbell explained the situation to his friend. Bamber said he'd be prepared to take the following day off work so that he could draw two thousand pounds from the bank at 9.00 a.m., and give it to Campbell. The Scotsman told Bamber that he would take a later train to London than usual, but would still have plenty of time to deliver the plastic bag to the Vernons at mid-day.

"I do think two's a bit on the steep side, Bill, old man," commented Bamber.

"These people are tough. They won't settle for less, but they're professional, all right."

"They'd bloody well better be, for that amount of money."

The Vernons were friendlier on seeing Campbell come into the Sawdust pub, carrying the plastic bag.

"Give it here, will you please," said Olive, smiling.

Campbell handed it over and returned her smile.

"Good on you, Mr Campbell, sir. Thank you," she said, and emptied the bag onto the table. She took fifteen minutes to count the notes, licking her fingers repeatedly as she did so.

"Thank you very much, Mr Campbell. That comes to two thousand pounds exactly. Thank you for bringing it so promptly. Will you have a drink?"

"Yes. Double whisky, please."

She called the order to the barman who brought the whisky to the table. Olive waited for Campbell to drink it.

"Nice meeting you, Mr Campbell. Do you want another?"

"Och, no thank you. It'll put me to sleep."

"Tell your friend we now know how to find his wife and her fancy fellow. He's a looker, all right, but we'll plug him for you good and proper. That's our trade."

Eddy was just about to leave his family to do the biggest hit job ever assigned to him. His mother called him to her side. "Now, you're going to get this one right, aren't you, Eddy, the way you got all the other jobs right? Just because there's a fortune to be got from it, it's no more difficult than the others."

Eddy had always had a masochistic crush on his mother. More than anything, he yearned to please her, although he had often experienced some twisted pleasure, mixed with tears when he did not.

The younger, less bright concierge, was on duty

when Eddy Vernon arrived at the Hogg's Back Hotel. He was short with red hair and was wearing a hearing aid.

The building was full of visitors about to attend a charity lunch when Vernon came into the lobby. Their entire conversation, delivered in a clattering mixture of base and piping voices, was about the Profumo Affair and the trial of Stephen Ward. It was that week that Ward was due to give evidence at the Old Bailey. Vernon had no idea who Stephen Ward was and, because he had only overheard snatches of conversation, he wondered whether this was the name Lt. Earnshaw was using.

"Can I help you, sir?" asked the young concierge, bored beyond oblivion with hearing perpetual references to Stephen Ward, as well as having nothing else to read about in the daily papers.

Unlike that of his brothers, Eddy's East End accent was scarcely apparent. This was because of his being closest to his mother, whose speech, although Cockney, was less noticeably so, due to her penchant for verbal gentility. Eddy was also an accomplished mimic and could take off any accent he heard.

"Morning," he said, raising his voice and mimicking a bogus American accent to disguise the remnants of his London East End vowels. "I want a room on the top floor, away from all this noise."

"What name is it, please?"

"Er.. Jones. Paul Jones."

"I think the noise will only be today, sir. Once the guests have left, it will be quiet all over. You don't need to confine yourself to those rooms. They're not very nice. They don't have proper windows, only skylights. They have attached bathrooms with showers. Our other rooms are a lot pleasanter."

"My pockets aren't lined with gold," said Vernon. "I need an inexpensive room. I don't mind having a skylight, and I can put up with a shower."

The concierge looked unhappy. The senior concierge, who was on leave for a week, would have been likely to reprimand him, for not allocating one of the costlier rooms to Vernon.

"All right. I'm happy for you to have a room on the top floor, if it's what you really want. So far, there are only two rooms occupied up there. There's a couple in one room, honeymooners, I think. Hardly ever come down. There's a young man in one of the other rooms. He's attending the lunch and is staying over for a day or two. There's one vacant room."

"I'll take it, then."

"All right. How long will you be staying?"

"I should think about three nights. How much

a night?"

"That comes to five pounds a night — fifteen in all."

"I'll pay now and get it behind me." Vernon reached into the inside pocket of his smart suit, paid for by one of Kelvin's jewellery thefts. He pulled out a crocodile-hide wallet which he himself had stolen. He counted the notes and laid them on the concierge's desk.

"Smart wallet you've got there."

Vernon was about to drop his Americanized accent, but checked himself.

"You think so? My aunt gave it to me. Birthday present."

Vernon lapsed into the crass behaviour which his family often hated him for.

"Do you know of a Lt. Earnshaw staying in the hotel?"

The concierge scratched his head with his pen.

"Earnshaw? That name's not familiar. When did he get here?"

"He could have been here for some time."

The concierge thumbed through some of the pages of his thick register, going back at least six weeks. He shook his head vacantly as he looked through the names, before reaching a conclusion, a gesture which infuriated Vernon.

"There've been no Earnshaws in here, sir. Is he

a friend of yours?"

"Yes. I know him. He said he sometimes stayed here. He said, if I was travelling this way, we might get together."

"Well, if he comes anywhere near here, I'll tell him you're in the hotel."

"Good. May I leave my car outside?"

"There's a carpark at the back of the hotel. It's a bit full, though."

Vernon collected his white Mini which he had left in the street. He had been paying for it by hire-purchase. He left it in the carpark, in a bay not far from Earnshaw's dusty Jaguar. He wiped the dust off the numberplate with the palm of his hand, just as Chris had done, and was satisfied the number was UUU 688. He went back to the hotel.

"Did you find somewhere to park?" asked the concierge.

"Yes. Could you please ask someone to take my suitcase up to my room? I'll take my briefcase later."

"Of course. You're in room 308. I hope it's not too cramped for you."

"Thank you. While you're at it, where's the bar?"

Vernon went to the bar and ordered a double whisky. He sat for a while, his mind busy. He studied the photographs entrusted to him in detail, and spent at least ten minutes, scrutinizing Earnshaw's face once more.

He decided to wait until 3.00 in the morning, before approaching the skylight, leading to Sally's and Earnshaw's room, and perhaps shooting his target then. Even a man of his low intelligence had realized that they had registered under another name. The whisky had exhausted him, but had by no means diminished the few instincts that his despairing family had instilled in its stupid youngest member. He walked towards the concierge.

"The key to room 309, please."

"No, sir! Yours is 308. God knows what antics you'd find going on in 309!"

"What antics?"

"I told you. The honeymoon couple are in 309. If you barged in there, you'd be turning the hotel into a French bedroom farce."

"Is that so?"

"And another thing, there's a full moon tonight. It will shine straight through all the skylights on the top floor, so I suggest you cover your eyes."

"Thanks. I'm so tired, I won't be coming down again. Could I please have a snack in my room at about 9.00 this evening?"

"Certainly. I'm sure that can be arranged. Do you want anything in particular? It's cold food only, though."

"Just ham sandwiches and beer will be OK."

"Is that all?"

"I said 'yes'."

"Then ham sandwiches and beer, it shall be."

"Do you mind if I ask you something?"

"Ask whatever you want."

"When you said all these people were leaving today, does that mean none of them will be spending the night here to sleep off their lunch?"

"None of them are booked in. Oh, except the young man on the top floor. The last of them should be out by tea-time at the latest. Why do you ask?"

"Because I'm worried about noise. I haven't been all that well. That's why my doctor told me to get away and stay somewhere quiet for a few days."

"You can be sure there'll be no noise, sir. The rooms on the top floor are the only ones that are occupied. In fact, we hardly ever have residents in the hotel."

Vernon looked puzzled. He took a cigarette from his (stolen) gold cigarette case and lit it with his (stolen) gold lighter.

"Cigarette?"

"No, thank you, sir. I don't smoke."

"How does your business survive if you hardly ever have anyone staying here?"

"We have regular functions, charity lunches, charity dinners, things like that. That's what brings in the bacon."

"Tell me," said Vernon, "if all the nicer rooms are vacant, why aren't you ever tempted to stay in one of them?"

"Because I'd get the sack if I were found out, obviously. If I want to keep my job, I have to stay in a small room in the basement."

"Do the staff stay in the basement as well?"

"Oh, you mean the cook, the porter and the cleaner? They don't stay in the basement, thank the Lord! They live away from the hotel.

"We still keep the porter on here, although we're hardly able to give him anything to do. My boss won't throw him out because he's been here for seven years.

"When he first came, more people stayed here, and there were fewer functions. My boss is a decent fellow. The porter's a nice chap, so he wants to keep him. His salary's not much. Occasionally, we give him the odd job to do, such as helping out when other staff are sick or on leave.

"He comes in to work, so called, every morning at 9.00 and spends a lot of his time, sitting in the staff room, doing the crossword. He always leaves at 5.00. Then, there's nobody else but me or the senior concierge on duty.

"I personally go to bed at 9.30 every night. It's best to warn you, just in case you thought this place was something like the Ritz."

"How strange, not that it bothers me," said Vernon. "You say you're alone when the porter leaves at 5.00, but you're not. What about the cook and the cleaner?"

"The cook leaves roughly the same time, unless there's a function. There's only cold food available in the evenings. As long as she knows in advance, she'll leave what you want aside for you. As for the cleaner, her hours are unpredictable. She comes in whenever she chooses in the mornings, to make the beds and clean the hotel. She has the rest of the day off and comes in at about 8.00 in the evening to turn down what few beds are being used. My boss likes her but I don't, particularly."

"Why?"

"She's a lazy, casual, laid-back woman. Most days, she doesn't even bother to do the bathrooms. She spends most of her time indulging in coarse, idle gossip. If someone wants dinner, either upstairs or in the dining room, she serves it. She likes to leave by 9.00, but in your case, she'll just have to leave a few minutes later."

"Why is she kept on?" asked Vernon.

"Because she's only paid a pittance. She probably does other jobs in between."

"Don't a lot of your customers resent not having a hot dinner?"

"Not at all. We always put our cards on the table, just as I am doing. We have to stay within our budget. Most people round here know this place is used mainly for public functions, and rarely for overnight visitors."

"So my neighbours, you and myself are the only people sleeping here?"

"Yes. Why on earth do you want to know all this, just out of interest?"

Vernon paused. He could almost feel Kelvin breathing down his neck, waiting for him to ask one question too many, before hitting him.

"I'm asking because ... well, it's not likely to happen, I'm sure. It's just that I'm a bit concerned there'd be a chance of me getting ill in the night. How would I be able to come all the way down to the basement, and get you to find me a doctor?"

"You're not likely to get ill, I hope, sir? With respect, this is a hotel, not a hospital. If someone stays here, it stands to reason they look after themselves. Besides, we've become much more modern than most hotels. There are telephones in all the rooms, now."

"As well as the rooms on the top floor?"

"Yes."

There was a long pause. Vernon was not graced with the art of obtaining vital information, without appearing to be an obsessive bore. The concierge remained friendly, just because he felt lonely and was in a talkative mood.

"I think I'll change my mind and accept one of your cigarettes, if I may, sir," he said.

"Of course." Vernon held out his cigarette case, and the concierge took a cigarette which he put in his mouth the wrong way round.

"No. You put the filter end in, first," said Vernon. "I'll light it for you. I don't think you've ever had a cigarette in your life, have you?"

"As a matter of fact, no."

Vernon inhaled deeply and the concierge copied him. He had no idea of the harsh pull one's first cigarette has on the back of one's throat, and made choking noises.

"You all right, mate?" Inadvertently, Vernon allowed his East End vowels to replace his makeshift American accent.

"Yes. I think so, now. I shan't be having one of those again," said the concierge, adding, "One great advantage of living in the basement, is that you don't hear a single sound in the rest of the hotel. Also, I sleep like a log which is lucky. Take where you're staying, for instance. Even if an H-bomb went off up there, I wouldn't hear it."

That was the only thing Vernon wished to be told. He thought it was worth having the exhausting conversation with the concierge, just to gain this information which was volunteered without him having to ask. He was also at an advantage, in that the unsuspecting concierge had almost as low an I.Q. as he did.

"That must be a great comfort to you, having all this nice peace and quiet. You look pretty tired, what with all these noisy people visiting. So am I. Thanks for the key. I'm going up for my rest now."

"Good afternoon to you, sir. I shall see to it that you have your ham sandwiches and beer at 9.00 this evening, as ordered."

Vernon was woken by the delivery of his snack by the over-talkative cleaner-come maid, who had been talking at length to the senior concierge, before his short holiday.

"Here you are, sir. I hope there's not too much noise up here. The concierge on duty at the moment said you liked peace and quiet."

"Yes. It's all right."

"Good. I expect you'll hear a lot of amorous noises later on, coming from the randy couple in 309. At it like rabbits, they are, all day and all night, too, I shouldn't wonder."

Vernon had all the information he needed and wanted to be alone. He was determined to do what he had to do, if only to avoid persecution by his bullying, overbearing family. He said,

"All right, all right. There's no need to be vulgar. I'd like to be left in peace, now. I'm very tired."

At about 10.00, Vernon heard loud giggling and moaning noises, combined with the sound of a creaking mattress, starting slowly and gathering speed like a Russian song. He kept himself awake until 3.00 in the morning. He took a pack of cards from the bottom of his suitcase, and calmed himself by playing Patience on his tiny, heavily stained bedside table. The noises stopped after three-quarters of an hour and were replaced by the sound of adoring, flirtatious voices. Then the noises started, once more. At about 1.00 a.m., there was silence.

Vernon felt saddened by the fact that he was being forced to ruin the happiness of a couple so hopelessly in love. He wanted to run away and go into hiding, and it was only his loyalty towards his mother, which prevented him from doing so.

The glare of the moon, shining straight at his face through the uncurtained skylight, had given him a headache. He began to wish he had no family, with the possible exception of his loving, but bludgeoning and demanding mother, whose photograph he had placed on the table by his rows of cards.

By 3.00, he could no longer bear the harsh moon piercing his eyes like a Lubyanka spot-light, any more than the sight of the eyes in his mother's photograph, which had stared straight at the camera when her picture was taken. They were hypnotic and he felt as if they were staring him out.

He turned his mother's photograph away from him. Then he changed into his tennis shoes and casual black running suit. He removed his Smith and Wesson from his briefcase. He covered his hands with surgical rubber gloves. The gun was unloaded, so he put six bullets into its freshly oiled chamber, and stowed it inside his pocket. He stood on the bed, raised his head and opened the skylight, before swinging his weight onto the roof.

He moved a few inches and advanced towards the skylight over room 309, ten feet away, where the noises had come from. He bent over it to see if he could ease it open, but found it was locked. He took a breaking and entering tool from his pocket and lifted it a few inches.

The moon enabled him to see what his mother and brothers wished him to see. Sally and Earnshaw were sleeping soundly. Sally's long peroxide hair was loose and her head rested on Earnshaw's chest. Both lovers had half smiles on their faces which corresponded identically with the photographs Vernon had been shown.

Vernon focused his Smith and Wesson on Earnshaw's forehead. He inserted the index finger of his right hand into the trigger guard and was about to bend it.

Suddenly, a horrible pain, both physical and psychological, surged through him. For a moment, he despised the mother he had always adulated. Had he bent his finger, he would have killed Earnshaw outright, but it dawned on him how morally wicked and cowardly it would be to kill someone who was asleep.

Also, it was only at this point that it suddenly crossed his muddled and disordered mind, that the other man, said to be occupying a nearby room, would be alerted by the shot, and possibly call the police.

It was not only his mother he despised at that moment. He felt hatred and disgust for himself, because he had gone so far as to actually point the gun at the sleeping Earnshaw's forehead, with intent to fire. He knew that his ruthless brother, Kelvin would have bent his finger then, and he realized, not without satisfaction, that he was a better man than he. He decided to wait for another opportunity to kill Earnshaw, but only provided he was awake, and had a chance of moving his head on seeing the barrel of the gun.

The task ahead of him saddened him even more as he returned to his room. He unloaded his Smith and Wesson, a possession he had once loved, but had come to hate, just like his family, in particular his brothers, who had robbed and scraped to supply him with it.

He put the six bullets into a small, leather box, containing other bullets. He wrapped the gun in a polythene bag and put both the gun and the box in the bottom of his briefcase, which he snapped shut before tapping out the numerical code, 100623. He put the briefcase in the cupboard which he locked.

He removed all his clothes and washed himself at the small, cracked, primitive basin in the bathroom. He took a few swigs from the king-sized bottle of whisky, which he had left on the floor by his bed, but the whisky failed to relax him and caused his headache to return. He turned onto his stomach, swore obscenely and bit into his pillow. It was only his despairing tears which helped him to sleep.

He hoped in vain that he would be able to sleep until 11.00 the next morning. At 10.00, he was woken by the sound of running water. His immediate reaction was to assume there had been a storm. It was not long before he realized it was something more worrying, and likely to thwart his plans.

He leapt out of bed and noticed that a flood of water was coming under his door. He told himself that the flow was temporary, but by the time fifteen minutes had passed, it was still running and the floor of his room was drenched. He didn't bother to dress and wrenched open the door.

He suspected the water was overflowing from a shower which had not been turned off. He walked through a small recess area and banged on the door of room 307, which the concierge had told him a young man was staying in. He became even more infuriated when he heard no answer.

He threw his weight against the door, bringing it down after three heaves. He noticed that the bed had been made, and the room cleaned and tidied. He followed the sound of the running water to the bathroom door and banged on that as well. He got no answer and forced it open.

He took one look at the scene before him, and was flabbergasted by the sight of a man, aged about twenty, sitting on the lavatory with its lid closed. He had frizzy brown hair and was thin and spindly in build. He was naked apart from an old Etonian tie which was tightened at the neck. The other end of the tie was attached to a broken pipe, leading to the cistern above the lavatory.

The man had been responsible for the flood and the gush of water into Vernon's room. He was a homosexual, and had tried to hang himself, because his male lover had gone home with another man whom he had met at the charity lunch the day before, instead of agreeing, as he had promised, to spend a few days with him on the top floor of the hotel.

"What the bloody hell do you think you're doing?" shouted Vernon. His anger was much more fiercely directed against his family, than against the pathetic, broken wreck who sat before him. To his astonishment, the man extended his hand.

"Chandler's the name. Tony Chandler," he muttered.

Vernon hated homosexuals because of the manner in which he had been conditioned by his brutal brothers, and the idea of having to touch one, if only on the hand, revolted him. He forced himself to shake Chandler's hand out of politeness.

"Jones. Paul Jones. You've got a repulsively limp handshake. Perhaps you'd care to explain why you've flooded this hotel. Do you normally go round flooding buildings as a habit, or is this just a hobby in which you like to indulge whenever the fancy takes you?"

Chandler began to cry.

"I tried to hang myself because I want to die," he said.

"I should think a lot of other people wish you'd die, too. Why did you have to do it this way? Why couldn't you go home and cut your wrists? Why should you want to die in any case? Are you on the run? Are you in debt? Have you just lost a close relative? Answer my questions, will you!" shouted Vernon.

"Please don't shout at me. I can't bear it. The man I've lived with for two years, doesn't love me any more," whispered Chandler.

"I'm not surprised. I expect you flooded his bloody house as well. No wonder he doesn't love you."

Vernon heard footsteps. He turned round and noticed that the hotel porter was standing just behind him. He had rushed upstairs to find out what had caused the flood, after finding that the kitchen was awash with gushing water.

"What's going on in here?" he asked mildly. "Why are you both naked?"

"I'm in love with a man who doesn't love me any more," bleated Chandler in a pitiful, half-witted tone.

"Are you referring to the man with you?"

"No. Someone else."

The porter noticed that the flow of water had stopped as the cistern was empty.

"I'm calling the police. Homosexuality is illegal," he said.

It had not occurred to Vernon before, that his nakedness in the presence of another naked man, would put him in such a compromising position.

Rage surged through him again because the delay was distracting him from his duty. He grabbed the porter by the scruff of his neck, lifted him from the floor and banged his head against the wall.

"Accusing me of being a bloody queer, are you?" he bellowed. "I was asleep. I was woken by water flooding into my room. It was an emergency. How do you expect me to have found time to dress? I had to rush out of my room to find out where the water was coming from. That's how I found this fellow."

He eased the porter onto the floor.

"I'm calling the police, now," the porter muttered.

Vernon took a towel from the floor and picked him up a second time. He carried him through Chandler's bedroom and threw him out into the corridor. He put the towel round himself and came out with him, quietly closing the bedroom door behind him, leaving it on the latch.

"Perhaps I was a little sharp with you earlier," he said, making an effort to sound apologetic and reasonable. "I don't know that man. I'd never met him before, until a few minutes ago. It's not his fault he's a homosexual. It probably runs in his genes.

"Believe me, I hate them as much as you do, but this man is tormented. It's help the poor fellow needs, not truncheons. Why can't you forget the whole thing ever happened? It would only mean you'd have to waste your time making a statement and standing up in court, submitting yourself to quite nasty cross-examination by his barrister. What he needs is the milk of human kindness.

"I can tell by your face that you're seeing sense in my words. I'll look after him. I'll cheer him up. I'll take him for a drive."

The porter was baffled and confused, and at the same time relieved by his inner decision not to interrupt the pleasant laziness of his routine, by calling the police. Vernon had no idea what he was thinking. He took a chance.

"Just wait here a moment, will you?"

The porter said nothing. He waited out of curiosity.

Vernon returned fully dressed within five minutes. He took out his wallet and handed a bank note to the porter.

"I've had enough of this. Do you understand?"

The porter still said nothing. Vernon wanted to kill him there and then, for failing to let him know where he stood with him.

"Take this, will you," he said, trying to control his temper. "Here's ten bob. Now clear off. I've not been well lately and my doctor has ordered me to rest. I don't want any further disturbance from you. If I want your services, I'll ring for them."

"Why, thank you, sir!" said the porter. "You won't be getting any trouble from me. I give you my word. After I've mopped up all the water which leaked, I'd be happy to mind my own business."

Vernon withdrew into Chandler's bedroom and stormed into the bathroom. He grabbed hold of his hair and wrenched his naked body from the lavatory seat.

"As for you, Chandler, you can stop attracting attention to yourself and wasting other people's time. If you want to die, die somewhere else, well away from me. Solve your own problems!"

Vernon went back to his room. He had no idea that Chandler had overheard him speaking kindly about him to the porter. The walls of the rooms were so thin, that someone as far away as the bathroom, could easily hear words spoken in the corridor.

Chandler overlooked Vernon's outburst of foul temper, and had taken note of his words "The poor fellow needs help, not truncheons". The effete, suicidal desperado was filled with hope that Vernon might try to befriend him after all. He had a sudden urge to speak to his jilting lover, but was unable to summon the courage to ring him up. He put on an effeminate, pink bathtowel dressing gown. Then he left his room, walked through the dividing recess area and knocked on Vernon's door.

Vernon knew that the events of the last hour had made it inappropriate for him to try to kill Earnshaw. The cleaner could soon be arriving to do their room and the porter was wandering about in the hotel. It was also possible that the concierge would hear the shot from his desk. Chandler, too, would hear the shot. The only suitable time for the assassination would be about 11.00 at night, when the pair would be awake, active and too preoccupied with each other to suspect Earnshaw's fate.

Vernon went back to sleep, and was livid when someone knocked on his door half an hour later.

"What the hell do you want?"

"It's only me, Tony Chandler. It was so kind of you to stop the porter calling the police. I'm really touched. Please let me in. I want to ask you another favour."

Vernon thought, if erroneously, that another kindly act towards this man, would send him away, satisfied.

"I suppose I'd better let you in. This is the last time I'll help you."

Chandler sat down on the bed. His cheap perfume nauseated Vernon.

"Well, what is it?"

"Will you ring up my friend for me? I haven't the guts to do it myself."

"I'll telephone no-one!" shouted Vernon. "Sort your problems out yourself. Go away."

Chandler slunk back to his room, angry with Vernon for being unfriendly and unco-operative. He picked up a heavy armchair, carried it to the door dividing the two rooms, and dropped it from a height, causing Vernon's sleep to be disturbed a third time.

Vernon wrenched open the door, thinking that the act of making a 'phone call on Chandler's behalf, might stop him pestering him.

"All right, Chandler. What's your friend's number?"

Chandler sat down on the bed next to Vernon and jumped up and down like a pubescent school-girl.

"Aldershot 6198," he gasped.

Vernon called the operator and asked for the number. A man with a bubbly, high-pitched voice answered.

"What name is it, Chandler?" rasped Vernon.

"Philip."

"May I speak to Philip, please," said Vernon.

The man answering the 'phone had a bizarre conversational habit of saying "yes" after every sentence he uttered.

"He's gone out to get some nice sticks of rock and straw hats for sitting on the beach, yes! Simply dastardly weather. We can't abide the heat, either of us, yes!"

Chandler knew Philip had not gone out. He heard him speaking to his friend, and snatched the 'phone from Vernon.

"I want you both to know that I've just tried to hang myself!" he shouted. "The only thing stopping me was that I was too heavy for the pipe leading to the lavatory cistern."

Something broke within Vernon. He snatched the receiver from Chandler's hand and slapped his face. He made a spontaneous decision to murder Chandler before shooting Earnshaw.

"Why are you doing this to me?" he asked with tears in his eyes. "What have I ever done to you? Let's just be friends without you pestering me like this. I know you've been hurt. Why don't you get dressed? Come back in about twenty minutes and I'll take you out for a nice drive. That will take your mind off all this, won't it? There's some lovely countryside around here. I have to warn you, though, that it will only be a short outing as I've got a business appointment in the hotel before lunch."

"Ooh, Mr Jones. Wouldn't that be nice? Aren't you kind? See you in twenty minutes, then. I appreciate your need to get back in good time."

Sally and Earnshaw had recently finished another of their carnal episodes. They had heard most of the noises in the next room. Sally was crying.

"Who are those two men, Ben? They're scaring me to death?"

"Don't be ridiculous, you lovely blonde bombshell. They're just a couple of queers having an argument. Do you really think that if they wanted to kill me, they'd make all that noise in the next door room before doing so?"

Chandler re-appeared in half an hour's time. He had taken a lot of pride in his appearance. He was wearing a pink suit, a ruffled silk shirt and a pink handkerchief round his neck.

"You're ten minutes late," complained Vernon. "Don't you remember me telling you about my appointment?"

"Ever so sorry. I wanted to look my best for our drive."

The two men went down to the lobby. The concierge scrutinized them both and looked bewildered. He wondered what a masculine-looking man like Vernon was doing in the company of an undisguised homosexual.

They left the hotel and got into Vernon's white Mini. Vernon said nothing as they drove through the neat, pine-tree peppered countryside. It wasn't until they had covered two miles that he spoke.

"There's a beautiful, dense pine forest coming

up on our left, and look at that pretty lake," he said. "We can't drive in so we'll leave the car outside. Are you fond of forests?"

"Oh, yes!"

"Good. Let's get out and go for a walk. There's a path going right through the forest. I've been along it before. It's mysterious and exciting. You'll love it."

Chandler was beginning to think that Vernon was a possible replacement for Philip. As they walked along the path into the darkness, Chandler put his hand round his frustrated companion's waist.

Vernon gagged but made no comment.

"All right, Chandler, we're coming straight to the heart of the forest. It's the most secluded place we can possibly be in. We can do anything we like without being seen. Then we can call ourselves by our first names. Ha! Ha! I want you to turn away from me, just for a moment. I've got a surprise for you."

"Ooh, how perfectly lovely!" began Chandler. His soul had been transported from hell to paradise in a matter of hours.

Vernon straightened his right hand, and brought it down on the back of Chandler's neck, letting out a menacing *Kung-Fu* shout. He assumed his victim was dead so he didn't bother to check whether he was breathing.

He dragged him through the dense trees, almost a mile from the path. He removed fifty pounds from his inside pocket and covered him, as best he could, with fallen branches and foliage. He found his way to the path, walked back to his car and returned to the hotel.

The concierge giggled cheekily as he walked past the reception desk.

"What's happened to your friend?" he asked.

"I don't see that that's any of your business," said Vernon, "but if you must know, he had a call from the hospital to say his mother was dying. I offered to give him a lift. He doesn't have transport."

"That's strange. He's left his little bubble-car in the carpark."

"I know. He told me. He was in such a state, he couldn't find his keys. I'll have my lunch in the dining room today. I was hoping I'd have peace and quiet on the top floor, but I've been disturbed more than I would have wished. I don't know how much more I'm prepared to tolerate."

"Sorry to hear that, sir."

"I had this man going on about his mother, when I was trying to have a lie-in. He told me he was so upset that he'd tried to kill himself. All I want is to be left alone."

"Well, I'm sure you will be, if the gentleman's

had to rush to his mother's bedside. I suggest you order yourself a nice lunch, and have a rest afterwards. Apparently, today's speciality is steak and kidney pie, a bit hot for the season, but one of our best dishes."

"Thank you. I won't be coming down again, after I've had lunch, so could I have ham sandwiches and beer again at 9.00 this evening?"

After Vernon had eaten again at 9.00, he waited until 11.00. He took out his Smith and Wesson and pushed the six bullets into its chamber. He put on his tennis shoes, rubber gloves, and black running suit, as before. He got onto the roof via the skylight, and moved towards the skylight covering Sally's and Earnshaw's room.

He could hear the creak of the mattress, even through the closed skylight. Earnshaw was lying on top of Sally and was having violent, prolonged sex with her while she screamed in ecstasy.

Vernon eased the skylight open with his breaking and entering tool. He focused the gun's front site on the back of Earnshaw's head and held it steady. He relaxed his watch to make sure no-one was standing behind him, and in his subconscious, he thought fleetingly of the way in which Kelvin sometimes crept up behind him, when he was doing his target practice as an adolescent. He was satisfied that no-one was watching him, and pulled the trigger.

He had failed to look at his target a second time before doing so. Sally and Earnshaw had suddenly turned over and changed positions. He noticed her lustrous, peroxide blonde hair was drenched in blood, covering the whole of the back of her head and neck. Earnshaw was lying underneath her, screaming.

Vernon's hand shook so much that he feared he might miss Earnshaw from the roof, so he scrambled down the slope under the skylight leading into the room. Earnshaw looked him in the eye, his face contorted with grief and terror.

"Please! There's no need to kill me!" he shouted.

Vernon went closer to him. "Turn your head the other way," he commanded, so that the blood from the potential gunshot wound would be less likely to splash his clothing. Only inches separated the gun's barrel from Earnshaw's temple. Vernon fired once, killing Earnshaw outright.

He eased the Smith and Wesson into Earnshaw's limp right hand and closed it, to make it look as if the two lovers had had a suicide pact. He went into the bathroom to wash away the small amount of blood which had covered his clothes and shoes, by shooting Earnshaw at close range. He ran water from the tap over the soles of his shoes as a precautionary measure. He wiped the remaining traces of the blood from the tiled bathroom floor, with Kleenex tissues which he flushed down the lavatory.

He saw Earnshaw's tailor-made, navy blue blazer strewn on the floor. He knew he would have to go on the run, and recognized the need to steal yet a further sum of money, besides the fifty pounds he had removed from Chandler's inside pocket.

Earnshaw had five hundred pounds in his inside pocket. The vastness of the sum did not surprise Vernon. He assumed it would have been difficult for anyone in hiding for several weeks, to take the risk of leaving the hotel to draw money from a bank.

He pulled his weight up to the open skylight, got out and closed it gently behind him. He checked that his breaking and entering tool was in his pocket. He returned to the skylight covering his own room and let himself in.

The time was 11.30. The fact that he had killed both the lovers, when he had only been ordered to kill one, shocked him so deeply that he stood in the middle of his tiny room, shaking like an epileptic.

His standing convulsive fit lasted for ten minutes. He sat down on the bed, reached for the bottle of whisky on the floor and drank almost enough to knock himself out.

The liquor temporarily clarified his thoughts and eased his shock. He continued to sit on the bed, staring into space. He decided to take off his "working" clothes, and bundle them into a polythene bag. He went into the bathroom, rolled off his rubber gloves and flushed them down the lavatory. He then sat down on his bed once more, his mind busy.

He planned to pack his few personal possessions, namely his playing cards, his mother's photograph, and washing materials.

His next move would be to leave the hotel, and shave his head in his car with his electric razor. He considered it in his best interests to drive to the lake he had passed with Chandler, let the handbrake off and force the car into the water.

He thought the police might initially suspect he had committed suicide, once they had found the lovers' bodies and linked them with his disappearance. By this time, he hoped to be somewhere in London, as far away as possible from the East End.

He would then travel to the Pembrokeshire port of Fishguard and board a ferry bound for the southern Irish port of Rosslare. He planned to pose as an American tourist and travel round Ireland with his stolen riches, until the heat was off. He wanted to settle somewhere, either in Dublin or Cork, lost to his family and the Law.

He had two more swigs of whisky, to steady his nerves. He then took his locked suitcase and briefcase from the cupboard. Both had the same code number. He was convinced he knew the number to open the two cases, by heart. Indeed, he had used it so many times that, when sober, he could have remembered it if walking in his sleep.

He sat on his bed with the suitcase on his knee, and pushed the white, plastic digits backwards and forwards in turn. The alcohol had prevented him from remembering the number 100623. First, he tried 100622, to no avail. Then, he tried 100625. He was so inebriated that he could hardly read the small numbers. He began to panic and pushed the digits at random, 100621, 100629, 110623.

He knew there was only one course of action open to him which was to force the lock on the briefcase. It contained a small, loaded lady's gun for emergency use, enabling him to blow open the lock on the suitcase.

At least, the alcohol gave him superhuman strength. He inhaled deeply, clenched his fist over the briefcase lock and dragged it, with a violent movement, towards him.

He ripped off the uncut nail of the index finger of his right hand but was too drunk to feel the pain. He only realized what had happened when a warm, wet sensation on his thigh alerted him, and he noticed the blood was coming from his finger.

He pulled the small gun from the bottom of his briefcase and fired a single shot at the suitcase lock. He took a handkerchief from the suitcase and bandaged his finger with it, now aware of acute pain, which he forced himself to ignore.

He lifted his arms above his head so that he could remove the top part of his sports suit, but they froze.

Someone was knocking on his bedroom door.

It took him at least a minute to be able to answer.

"Who the hell is it? It's after mid-night!" he shouted, unable to disguise his breathing.

"It's me. Tony Chandler." His voice was a raised, peeved bleat.

Vernon was convinced that he had murdered Chandler and hidden his body in the forest earlier that day. He wondered whether it was excessive alcohol or a ghostly whine from the dead, which had started to dent his sanity.

He picked up his two cases and put them back in the cupboard. He dragged his dressing gown over his sports suit, hoping that his visitor would mistake it for a pair of pyjamas. He decided to let the man in, and if necessary convince him that someone else might have tried to kill him.

He opened the door. Chandler was standing outside with his torn pink suit and ruffled shirt covered in mud.

"Come in, you bloody fool! I've been wanting to give you a good hiding all day. You've taken advantage of my goodwill for longer than I'm prepared to tolerate. You really pissed me about this morning."

"I've pissed you about?" shouted Chandler.

"Keep your voice down. You're a selfish little man. There's a couple somewhere in this corridor, trying to get a night's sleep. Sit down on the bed. If you raise your voice higher than a whisper, I'm going to give you a good clout."

"Look here, Mr Jones, I think you hit me when we were on our walk. I woke up in horrible pain, I found myself under a pile of branches."

"You're drunk, Chandler," said Vernon. "I'll tell you what happened, before you accuse me of hitting you. When I met you first, you had tried to commit suicide because your friend refused to stay with you.

"Although I'm an exceptionally busy man, I took pity on you. I thought I might be able to cheer you up by taking you for a drive. You said you liked pine forests so I took you to one and we agreed to go for a short walk.

"I told you we couldn't be too long because I

had to be back here for an appointment. Do you remember that?"

Chandler was even more confused than he had been earlier. He wondered whether he had accused his rude, but kind-hearted benefactor, unjustly.

"Yes," he said quietly.

"We were walking down the path through the forest. You said you wanted to go through the trees to answer a call of nature. I said I'd wait for you. Do you remember that?"

"No. All I remember is — we were walking along and suddenly everything went blank."

"Are you taking any medication, Chandler?"

"Yes. The doctor gave me some blue pills to make me sleep."

"Let me tell you what happened," said Vernon. "You went off into the trees. I waited on the path for a quarter of an hour. There was no sign of you. In short, you just buggered off. You knew very well I was anxious to get back to the hotel. I went into the wood to look for you. I thought you might have deliberately tried to harm yourself because you were upset about your friend. I ran all over the place, shouting for you. I tried to find you for at least half an hour.

"In the end, I thought you were quite old enough to find your way back. I had to put my appointment first, so I went to the car and returned to the hotel.

"The first thing I did when I got here, was to ring the police. I didn't tell them you were queer. I just said you were upset about something and had disappeared into the forest. Incidentally, they said you were well-known in this area, but they told me they were sending out a search party all the same.

"I really don't know what more I could have done for you, Chandler. Everywhere you go, you seem to upset people."

"Whom have I upset?"

"I'll tell you who. You upset the porter here this morning. He spent hours clearing up the awful mess you made. No doubt, you upset your friend which is why he refused to see you any more. You certainly upset me. Not only that, you accused me of hitting you. By God, I wish I had!"

"Why was I buried under a pile of branches, then?" asked Chandler.

"How the hell should I know? It's possible the pills you take to sleep, make you sleepy during the day as well. You started to feel very tired. You probably crawled under some fallen branches to make a bed for yourself, although you knew I was waiting for you. That's why I said you were a selfish little man, and I meant it, too."

Vernon was satisfied with the plausible nature of his story. Whisky had always enabled him to lie so convincingly that even he believed he was telling the truth.

"Maybe, I was a bit harsh, Chandler," he began.

"Tony."

"Oh, sorry, Tony. You've had a pretty bad day, but I feel I can help you have a pleasant ending to it. Some whisky?"

Chandler swallowed almost half a pint from the king-sized bottle.

"Go easy on that stuff. It'll knock you out," said Vernon.

"How can you make the ending of my day pleasant?"

"Thinking about yourself again, I see. I'll tell you. There's an all night party, tonight. Most of the men there will be of your persuasion. I heard about it from someone in the bar. Would you like me to take you along?"

"Ooh, yes, Mr Jones, yes, please!"

"Paul. Do you know the geography of this corridor?"

"No. Not really."

"I'll explain. Your room's 307. Mine's 308. There's no-one in 309 but there's a couple in 310. Room 309 is never used."

"Why?"

"Because these special parties take place quite

often. There's a trap door in room 309 under the double bed. It leads to a lower attic room which is soundproofed."

"Oh, Paul, it sounds so exciting. Quite an adventure!"

"There's a double bed in room 309. The men in the room below will have been hard at it for hours and sometimes come up to lie down.

"There's another thing about this kind of party which will interest you. It's the done thing for everyone to wear gloves. It doesn't matter what kind of gloves, just gloves."

The half pint of whisky had sent Chandler into a happy, unsuspecting, incomprehensible dream.

"Why?" he asked, smiling as excitedly as a three-year-old child, about to be taken to a circus.

"Just to make the whole thing more mysterious and weird, I suppose," said Vernon. "There's a big bowl of purple hearts down there, too. Everyone helps themselves. Have you ever taken them?"

"No."

"I have. They cause you to have a feeling of euphoria which goes on for days. Have you got any gloves with you?"

"I never wear gloves in the summer."

"Not even for driving, to stop the sweat getting on the steering wheel?"

"I'm afraid not. Will they still let me in?"

"Yes, I should think so. I'm putting on my leather gloves. I won't stay long. When I leave, I'll give them to you. It will be my gift to help you forget our argument."

"Oh, thank you, Paul!"

"We should be starting off, now. I don't want to be there too long as I'm exhausted."

Vernon took his dressing-gown off and dragged his leather gloves on to his hands, allowing his bandaged right finger to protrude.

"What have you done to your finger, Paul?"

"Oh, I had to get something out of my suitcase. I couldn't remember the combination number, so I had to force it open. It cut right into my nail. There may be a bit of blood about, because of it."

"How nasty! Is it agony?"

"No, of course it isn't!"

"Don't you think you ought to get it properly seen to in hospital?"

"No, of course I don't! Don't be a drip."

"Do I have to change?"

"No. You look fine as you are. Better than the bloody Prince of Wales! Come on. Let's go."

Vernon helped Chandler through the skylight and onto the roof, holding his hand throughout.

"Beautiful stars," he remarked.

"Aren't they, just? Isn't this fun?"

Vernon said nothing. The skylight leading to

room 309 was looser than before, when it had been necessary to open it with a tool. Vernon pulled it open with his gloved left hand. He said,

"I'll go down the slope first, but I'll hold on to you to stop you falling. It will be easier if we face outwards. I'll hold my arms together across your chest. I expect your father did this to you when you were small."

"I feel so happy and safe, now," said Chandler.

"Good. Just slide down the slope. I've got you."

Once the two men were on the floor, Vernon hugged Paul and stroked his chest. He felt disgusted.

"Don't look behind you. Close your eyes and come with Uncle Paul." He turned Chandler round, facing the bed. "Just keep walking. I'm coming behind you."

"Dear, sweet Uncle Paul!" exclaimed Chandler, his whisky-sodden speech slurred, and his mind almost paralysed.

"Are your eyes still closed?"

"Yes, Uncle Paul."

"There's no need to call me 'Uncle Paul'. Just 'Paul' will do. We're walking towards the bed."

"Are you still behind me?"

"Yes, my boy. Keep those eyes closed. Once we get there, we'll give the bed a push to get to the trap door. We'll go through the trap door together and I want you to promise me not to open your eyes, before we get into the sound-proofed party room, and hear the music."

"I promise."

"Good boy."

"What's this horrible smell, Paul? It's like meat that's gone off."

"I can't smell anything, my boy. That drink's made your imagination run wild. You certainly didn't stint yourself. Just keep walking."

Vernon knew nothing about rigor mortis and was terrified it might have set in. He was so relieved to be able to ease the Smith and Wesson from Earnshaw's still limp hand, that he almost wept with joy. He realized his task would be less easy this time, because his injury to his finger, meant that he would have to use his left hand to shoot.

"Uncle Paul?" bleated Chandler.

"No, Paul," said Vernon brusquely. "What's the matter?"

"I think I want to be sick."

Vernon foresaw the ghastly consequences of this happening, as he wanted the scene to have the initial appearance of an inexplicable triangular suicide. Then it dawned on him that the presence of vomit in the room, might give the impression that the potential murderer's reason for killing the two others, had been inspired by over-indulgence in illicit drugs.

He thrust his left index finger into the trigger guard, and was jolted by the bulkiness of the leather glove. He wriggled it into a straight position, took a few steps backwards and pointed it at the back of Chandler's frizzy brown head.

"If you want to be sick, go ahead and be sick. I won't mind. You'll feel a lot better once it's up," said Vernon.

Chandler bent over and suddenly opened his eyes. He saw the back of Sally's head covered with half-dried blood, and the dead Earnshaw lying beneath her. He leant over the bed and gripped Sally's body to support himself. He was sick before he had a chance to scream. It was while he was being sick, and making things more difficult by the jerking movements of his head, that Vernon bent his finger and fired twice.

One bullet entered Chandler's neck and exited the other side, killing him. Vernon's left hand had become unsteady. The exceptionally surreal nature of the situation, made his whole body shake, and the only factor saving him from complete despair, was Kelvin's absence from the scene.

The second bullet, aimed at Chandler's head, whistled through his hair and penetrated the door of the wardrobe. Vernon opened Chandler's right hand, just as he had Earnshaw's, and closed his fingers on the gun. This time, he made absolutely sure he was dead.

It was only then that he realized that no forensic investigator would see his third victim's death as suicide. A suicidally caused gunshot wound would be unlikely, if almost impossible, to inflict via the back of the neck. He hoped in vain that the police called to the scene would be fractionally stupider than he. He knew exactly what his family meant when they told him he was stupid, and he felt belittled and ashamed.

He saw no point in covering his traces in the room, as the whole place was awash with blood. The only point in his favour was the fact that he had worn gloves while committing all three murders. That meant he had left no prints, either in room 309, or the bathroom.

He removed his shoes before leaving room 309. He closed the skylight just as he had before, and returned to his room. He rolled all his murder clothes, as well as the shoes, with the exception of his leather gloves, into a polythene bag as he had planned, and packed it, along with his other belongings. He took a shower and washed his hair before changing into the navy blue suit, matching tie and white shirt he had been wearing in the hotel.

He checked there were no traces of transmitted

blood in his bedroom and bathroom. He finished the bottle of whisky, and put the lady's gun in his inside jacket pocket.

Among the things in his suitcase, were three spare shirts, tooth cleaning materials, an electric razor, a packet of Gillett's razor blades, his mother's photograph and his leather gloves.

He brushed his hair and carried his cases down to the lobby. He noticed that the time, given on the clock on the wall above the concierge's desk, was just after 1.00 a.m. He took out his wallet and counted the money he had stolen from the jackets of his victims. It amounted to five hundred and fifty pounds.

He leant over the concierge's desk, picked up a ballpoint pen and tore a page from the notebook, which the concierge kept for taking telephone messages. He intended to cause as much confusion as he possibly could, aware that the police would arrive the following morning to question the concierge. He wrote a lengthy, bizarre letter, his handwriting only just legible after his alcohol intake.

To the concierge.
Sorry, I don't know your name. By the time you get this note, I will have buggered off out of your ghastly hotel.

I'm pissed off.

I'm a sick man and I only graced your establishment with my presence because my doctor in London ordered me to rest in respectable, quiet surroundings for three days.

You assured me that I would find these on the top floor. Did I? Bloody hell, no! The first night my sleep was disturbed by a shrieking, fornicating couple.

On my first morning, while I tried in vain to make up for my sleep deprivation, a horrible little man woke me up on three occasions. On the first two occasions, he asked me to make telephone calls on his behalf to some other dreadful man about his failed suicide attempt and desire to die. On the third occasion, when I was feeling so tired and ill, I thought my heart would give out, he harassed me yet again and forced me to listen to him talking about his bloody mother.

He just wouldn't stop. He actually thought I'd want to hear the intricate details of where her cancer had started and what other organs it had spread to. "Ovary, bowel, pelvis, liver, brain!" he kept shouting, repeating himself over and over again, using me like a blessed punch ball.

He also flooded my room, I suspect

deliberately because he is mentally deranged. Through the milk of human kindness, I drove him to see his mother. I hoped he'd be away for a few days, waiting for her to die.

I prayed that I would have a decent night, but he came to my room and woke me up sometime after mid-night. He was very drunk and waving a bloody great revolver around. He said he was prepared to kill anyone he could find because his mother had finally died, and her death made him angry.

Ill and tired, though I was, I talked him out of it. He said he was going to be sick so I ordered him to his room.

Not only that, as I hovered between sleep and wakefulness before his return to the hotel, I heard shooting in the street and the loud noises of a car backfiring.

I'm not prepared to sit the rest of the night out. I know he'll come back early in the morning, pestering me.

Because you deceived me about the peace I would receive here, I must ask you to send me a refund of the fifteen pounds I paid you on my arrival.

As I barely have any money at all (I've had to spend most of it on my doctors), I demand that you send me an immediate repeat immediate

cheque to me at the following address:
The Sun Inn
Weymouth
Dorset.
   I am an honourable person and as I have been raised to pay debts when they are due, I expect honourable behaviour in others.
Yours sincerely,
Paul Jones, Esq.
PS: I have forgotten to remind you of my lineage, incurring my extreme respectability. My mother is a senior nurse who devotes her life to healing the sick. My late father, God rest his soul, was a worthy and deeply religious policeman.

Vernon read his letter twice, and was amused by the lies it contained. He was satisfied that its perplexing tone and inordinate length would both confuse and waste the time of the concierge, and any police investigators called to the hotel. He folded it in half, wrote the words "Concierge" on the outside, and placed it on the desk with the ballpoint pen lying across it.

He briefly looked at the clock, and noted that the time was already 1.40. He carried his suitcase and briefcase out of the hotel to his Mini, and put them on the passenger seat.

He noticed that the only other car in the carpark was Earnshaw's green Jaguar, which had gathered another layer of dust since he had last seen it. The sight of it reminded him of every crass mistake he had made, and caused another wave of shame and personal worthlessness to surge through him. Tears filled his eyes as he thought of the mother he had betrayed by his incompetence, and whom he knew he would never be able to face again.

He was feeling a little less befuddled, and more despondent, now that the effects of the whisky were wearing off, but he was relieved that he had managed to make logical plans for his escape, before leaving the hotel.

He leant over to the passenger seat and took out his electric razor, with his left hand while his right hand, its index finger throbbing with intolerable pain, focused the car's mirror on his face. His left hand was not agile enough to shave off his thick black hair, so he held the razor in his right hand, carefully bending all his fingers over it, except his index finger which he held straight in the air.

It took him ten minutes to make his head completely bald. When he looked at his reflection in the mirror, he thought, for a fleeting moment, that someone else's face was staring at him, and jumped with terror.

He engaged gear but his foot was shaking so

violently, that he pushed the accelerator too hard, and crashed into Earnshaw's Jaguar.

"I suppose I don't have to leave a note of my name and address on his windscreen, now," he said, half to himself and half out loud. He giggled nervously and somehow, his laughter strengthened his spirits and determination to escape, with fractionally more practicality and intelligence than he had displayed in the course of his duty.

He eased the Mini out of the carpark and drove to the lake near the pine forest, in which he had walked with Chandler. He took advantage of the fact that there was a fairly steep slope leading to the water. He drove as far as the top of the slope. He took from his suitcase, the polythene bag containing his murder clothes, with his breaking and opening tool, in one of the pockets, and tennis shoes.

He opened the boot with difficulty, as his aching bandaged finger was in his way. He screwed up the polythene bag, and pushed it to the back of the boot. He got into the car and opened all four windows, to enable it to sink more quickly.

It was only then that it crossed his slow-working mind, how essential it was to check the depth of the lake. For this purpose, he would need a long stick, he told himself.

He took his torch from the boot. It radiated a small amount of light, but enough to guide him into the forest, to find a long stick or an equally long broken branch.

It did not take him long to find a loose stick on the ground, about ten feet long. It had fallen off one of the trees during a winter gale.

He carried it back to where he had left the car. He took off his clothes and watch, and slid down the slope, into the water. It was so unexpectedly deep, that it almost came over his head. He did not need the stick to tell him that his head and shoulders, and part of his chest, were taller than the roof of the Mini.

He removed his cases, made sure that all his clothes were on land, eased himself behind the wheel of the car, and revved up the engine. He reversed up the slope and continued for about thirty yards on the flat, dry grass. He then engaged first gear and pushed the accelerator until it touched the floor.

He was in the lake in a matter of seconds. He found his way out of the driver's open window to the surface of the water.

He swam a few yards back to the shore. He put on his clothes and watch, and suffered another agonizing pain in his finger. As the handkerchief was now loose, he took it off and put it in his trouser pocket. He told himself that the wound would heal more quickly in the fresh air and that the pain would ease in a day or two.

The fullness of the moon enabled him to watch the Mini sinking. He was surprised by the length of time it took and waited, feeling more and more depressed by the appalling mess he had left behind him, as well as his urgency to get to London.

He waited patiently for the roof of the Mini to become submerged. He made sure he had left no evidence of his presence. He checked that there weren't any loose papers or other incriminating material, that could have floated through the open car windows, up to the water's surface.

He picked up his two cases, and walked briskly for a few miles, until he reached the main road leading to London. He looked at his watch. The time was 3.25 a.m. He stood on the concrete verge on the left hand side of the road and waited.

He expected the road to be deserted at this time. The pain in his finger took his mind off his anxiety, and in a strange way, helped him to be patient.

Two lorries passed him in quick succession. Fifteen minutes later, a car, driven by a woman, roared past him at 100 m.p.h. There was nothing on the road for at least twenty minutes after that.

Vernon began to despair of reaching London by sunrise. He wondered who would find the bodies of his victims and when. The concierge told him that the cleaner's times of arrival at the hotel were unpredictable, and Vernon concluded that she tended to be a latecomer.

He thought of what might happen if she suddenly veered from her tardy routine, and decided to impress her colleagues by arriving unusually early. Once she found the bodies, it would only be a matter of minutes for the police to arrive and the heat to be on him.

His breathing became laboured, and he felt faint, hungry and frightened. He sat down on the concrete verge. He thought of getting out his cards and playing Patience to calm his nerves, which would have been easy in the total absence of breeze, but he decided that doing so, would attract unwanted attention to himself.

At that moment, he wanted, more than anything else in the world, to sleep, but he knew this luxury would be denied him for at least a day or two, if he were to survive.

He sat with his legs stretched in front of him and leant back, supporting himself with his arms. He drifted into sleep. He saw his mother alternating between wringing her hands and weeping, and slapping his face. He felt Kelvin kicking him in the ribs while Alan sat on his haunches, jeering. He saw the two happy lovers hugging each other, unaware of the forthcoming robbery of their happiness.

They were at a bus-stop. A bus travelling at a high speed, with a noisy engine was coming from a distance. It slowed down and its engine became quieter until it came to a halt.

Vernon felt someone tapping him on the shoulder. He woke, startled. Standing in front of him, was a man roughly his height, aged about 35. He was bald, despite his youth. He was wearing a pin-striped suit, waistcoat and watch chain. He owned a polished dark grey Rover which he had moved to the side of the road.

Vernon shifted his position abruptly like an animal about to be cornered.

"It's all right, sir. No need to be frightened of me. I'm not going to hurt you." The newcomer, who had been travelling on the London road, had a soft, gentle, Southern Irish accent.

"I'm OK," said Vernon. "I missed the late night train. I've been here for hours. I want to go to London."

"London?" said the man. "That's where I'm going. Let me give you a lift. You look worn out. What's your name? Finbar O'Cassidy's mine." He extended his hand, but Vernon responded by waving his hand in the air.

"I'm Ian Moore. I'm pleased to meet you."

"Good. Now, we're friends," said the kindly Irishman. "Let me help you into the car. I'll put your luggage in the boot."

"Thanks." Vernon got in and sat stiltedly in the passenger seat.

"You haven't had anything to eat for a while, have you?"

"No."

"Would you like to share my sandwiches with me? Ham and cheese, I've got, and a nice hot flask of tea."

O'Cassidy handed half of his sandwiches to Vernon, who bit into them and swallowed them in noisy gulps. It was only after he had finished that he muttered the words "Thank you very much," in rather an ungracious tone.

"Do you feel a bit better now, Mr Moore?"

"Yes. Yes, I do, thanks."

"Have some of my tea."

"No, thanks."

"Mind you, I don't live in England. I live in Ireland, out in the country. I expect you can tell by my accent."

"Yes. Yes, I can," said Vernon. "It's very distinctive."

"I'm only over here for my holidays. I've made a lot of money in Ireland. I own a string of betting shops and I breed horses. My poor wife died two months ago. I keep myself as busy as I can. Oh, God, do I miss her! Her name was Mary. I loved her sorely."

"Oh, dear, I'm so sorry," the murderer forced himself to remark.

Neither man spoke for ten minutes. Vernon was the first to break the silence.

"Are you enjoying your holiday, Mr O'Cassidy?" he asked.

"I'm not exactly enjoying it. It's only partly taking my mind off Mary's death. I've come over here to watch the trial."

"Oh? You mean one of the horse trials?"

O'Cassidy's tear-stained face suddenly lit up.

"No! You must know what I'm talking about. The biggest scandal trial of the century. The trial of Stephen Ward."

"Stephen Ward? The name's familiar," said Vernon. "Is he a serial killer or something?"

O'Cassidy swerved a few feet over the road.

"Sure, I'm astonished you don't know. I'll tell you. Stephen Ward's a saucy, sex-obsessed, high society osteopath — back specialist, that is. He knows nearly everyone in London, from top politicians to the very dregs of the gutter. He keeps company with pot-smoking West Indians, street-walkers and even knows Sir Winston Churchill and the Duke of Edinburgh."

"Why's he on trial?" asked Vernon impatiently.

"Because he introduced a lady to a Russian spy

and the Minister for War. He caused what was seen as a security risk. They couldn't prove he was a spy, so they charged him with living on prostitutes' immoral earnings."

"It sounds a really boring case to me," said Vernon irritably.

"No. That's where you're wrong. Once a Tory War Minister confesses he's been sleeping with a woman, who's also been sleeping with a Russian spy, that's the end of what was once a perfect Tory government. When I was a child, Mr Moore, my mother used to take me on her knee and say 'Remember one thing, son. England's difficulty is Ireland's opportunity'. The saying goes back for hundreds of years."

"What are you talking about? You're not making any sense."

O'Cassidy overlooked Vernon's rudeness.

"Of course, what my mother said, has never effected me. I'm not a political man. I'm not all that interested in my country's history, either. I'm more interested in what goes on in London, than at home. My greatest passion is horses. I love horses more than anything else in the world."

They came to a red light. There was still barely any traffic on the road. O'Cassidy drove through it.

"You shouldn't have gone through a red light," said Vernon. "It's not right to break the Law."

"No matter, Mr Moore, no matter. I've told you about me. Tell me something about yourself, that is if you wish to. Where are you from? Why are you so keen to get to London?"

"I was born in London but I live near Aldershot," said Vernon, in staccato blasts. "I've got two twin sons, aged eight. When they're not at school, they are looked after by a nanny. My wife walked out on me. She went to London. I'm on my way there to find her and talk her into coming home."

"I'm sorry, Mr Moore. Do you know where in London she went to?"

"Yes. Kensington way. She's gone to stay with her sister."

"Then let's hope you get her back soon. I know what loneliness is, Mr Moore. Why don't you cheer yourself up? Come and watch the trial with me, eh?"

"Where is it?"

"At the Old Bailey. It's such a popular case because of all the sordidness in it, that there's a queue nearly a mile long outside the court. Ward's in the middle of giving his evidence today, so the queue will probably be longer."

Vernon thought O'Cassidy was raving mad.

"When does the hearing start?" he asked courteously, to make up for his former rudeness.

"10.00. We'll be in London by 7.30."

"Will that give us enough time to get in?"

"Good God, no! To get in to hear Ward, you have to spend two days and two nights sleeping on the window-ledges. The public gallery can't hold more than about forty people. But I'm no fool. I know a way round it. There are one or two men, always at the front of the queue. They've slept there for two nights on the window ledges. They haven't come for the trial. They come to sell their places to the well-off, who aren't prepared to wait for two nights to get a seat."

Vernon said nothing. He rested his head on the back of his seat, now wide awake. He closed his eyes to give O'Cassidy the impression he was sleeping but his mind, now entirely free of the muddled effects of liquor, was busy.

He knew that, once in London, O'Cassidy would be averse to parking in a street, because of the shortage of parking spaces in the City, and the problem of feeding and re-feeding a parking meter. He suspected the streetwise Irishman would favour a multi-storey carpark.

At 7.40, O'Cassidy tapped Vernon on the shoulder.

"We're here now, Mr Moore. 'Twas a good, clear run and I'm glad you've had some sleep."

They were driving round Smithfield Meat

Market and past St Bartholomew's Hospital. On the wall of the hospital, to the left of the main gate, was thick red graffiti, ten feet high. The message, obviously written in a spirit of passionate anger, read,

THIS HOSPITAL IS AS CORRUPT AS CALIGULA'S ROME.

"Do you know what that means?" asked Vernon.

"Yes. It's been in all the papers. That hospital is notorious for its treatment of its staff. A nice, respectable girl worked for a consultant there for five years. She worked like a pit pony and even came in at weekends.

"One day, a man she loved, drowned. The consultant was jealous of her love for him, and trumped up false charges against her. He lied to the administrators, saying she was mad, that she had started fires, and that she had forged doctors' signatures on medical reports. She was sacked and was so grief-stricken that she didn't have the strength to defend herself."

"What happened to her?"

"She jumped under an underground train. No-one round here will ever forget the injustice of it all."

"There are some particularly evil people in this world, of course," remarked Vernon.

O'Cassidy indicated right and crossed the road to West Smithfield's multi-storeyed underground carpark, which had only recently been built.

He eased his Rover down a stony slope and inserted his temporary ticket into a slot, just before the barrier rose. The carpark attendant was sitting in a wooden box, his head buried in a newspaper. He didn't notice the car go by.

"It won't be long, now, will it, Mr Moore? The Old Bailey's a five minute walk away from here. I'm going down to the lowest storey, away from anywhere. That way, there's less risk of my car being stolen. Besides, I love the bowels of the earth. They remind me of the teacher at my school who told us stories about the rebels hiding underground, during the 1916 Uprising."

The bottom storey was deserted. The two men got out. Vernon put his hand on O'Cassidy's shoulder.

"I want to repay your kindness, Mr O'Cassidy. I've got a present for you in my luggage. Is your boot locked?"

"No."

"Good. I'd like you to walk over to that wall and close your eyes and turn your back to me. It's part of the surprise."

"Sure, this is a great honour."

He walked to the wall and stood facing it,

smiling like a child, as he waited for his present.

Vernon took his suitcase out of the boot, and put it on the concrete surface. He opened it and removed his Gillet razor blades from his toilet bag, and his leather gloves. He took the loaded lady's gun from his inside pocket and put the gloves on.

Although the ache in his right index finger had lessened a bit, he had another sharp, stabbing pain as he pulled on his right glove. He eased his finger gently into the trigger guard and put the razor blades into his pocket with his left hand.

He walked towards his target with a casual, springing gait.

"You can turn round, now, Mr O'Cassidy."

O'Cassidy was touched by the fact that his travelling companion had taken so much trouble to please him. It took him two seconds to notice that a gun was being pointed at his left temple, its barrel pressing heavily against his skin.

"Don't move, don't speak and don't scream, Mr O'Cassidy. If you do as I say, no harm will come to you. Take off your clothes, all of them, and let them fall on the concrete on your right hand side."

O'Cassidy obeyed, looking profoundly hurt. There were tears in his eyes.

"Take off your briefs and your socks."

O'Cassidy took them off and dropped them on the top of the pile.

"And the gold watch and signet ring."

O'Cassidy felt sad rather than frightened. A tear trickled down his cheek. Vernon was so ashamed of what he had to do in order to survive, that he averted his eyes from the tear, as he feared that he, too, were about to cry.

"Please, Mr Moore. Let me keep the watch. Mary gave it to me for my birthday, not long before she died. You can have everything I own, including the car, but please, I beg of you, if you have any mercy at all, don't take the watch. It means more to me than I can say in words."

Vernon felt his throat tighten. He bit his lip and swallowed hard.

"I thought I told you not to speak," he said, avoiding eye contact with O'Cassidy. "Sorry. You can't keep the watch. If you speak again, I'll have to shoot you."

O'Cassidy wept openly, but stopped in amazement when he saw Vernon taking his wallet from his inside pocket, before removing all his clothes, as well as his watch and the St Christopher medallion round his neck. He put his watch on O'Cassidy's left wrist, removed his medallion and draped it round his neck, still managing to hold the gun. He took the razor blades from his pocket and dropped them on the concrete.

"Now, do everything I say and you won't get

hurt. Bend over. Pick up my clothes and put them on. This gun's loaded. One false move on your part, and I'll fire, although, because of your kindness, I won't want to."

O'Cassidy's trembling hands pulled on Vernon's clothes, starting with his briefs and socks. His shoes were fractionally too small for him. He stooped to tie up the laces and Vernon bent over, keeping the gun pressed to his temple. He picked up the razor blades, which he had removed from the pocket of the trousers O'Cassidy was now wearing.

"Good man," he said. "There's just one more thing I'm going to ask you to do."

O'Cassidy remained silent as instructed. He eyed Vernon questioningly, still horribly hurt.

"Take one of these razor blades out of its case. Hold it in your right hand between your thumb and index finger. Then hand it back to me, with its case, and close your eyes."

"I don't mind if you do kill me, Mr Moore," O'Cassidy said, "I've nothing to live for. I want to be reunited with my beloved Mary."

Vernon held the razor blade and, with a sudden movement of his right hand, he cut deeply into O'Cassidy's throat, bringing the razor blade from below his right earlobe to his left. As he hit the jugular artery, a heavy, pulsating jet of blood gushed in Vernon's direction, narrowly missing him.

"Lie down on your back, now," he said gently.

O'Cassidy was so weak from loss of blood that he lay down willingly.

"I'll stay with you until you go, Mr O'Cassidy," said Vernon kindly. "It wouldn't be right to let you die alone. Also, there'd be the risk that someone might find you and try to save your life. Of all the people I've murdered, you will be the only true genuine gentleman I've dispatched into the next world."

"I've never understood why English people always have to be so unkind," whispered O'Cassidy.

He raised his head with an effort. In a few seconds, it hit the concrete with a thud. His eyes were open and staring and focused on Vernon, who closed them reverently with his gloved hand, and burst into tears.

The river of blood from O'Cassidy's body flowed through the loose stones on the concrete, away from the place where he had been ordered to leave his clothes. Vernon dragged them hurriedly onto his body, starting with the gold watch and the matching signet ring. He put on O'Cassidy's pinstripe suit, including the waistcoat and watch chain. The fact that his victim wore two watches gave Vernon the impression that he had been a meticulous time-keeper.

He picked up the case containing the razors, put his victim's wallet and the gun in the inside pocket of O'Cassidy's jacket, threw his suitcase into the boot of the Rover, and moved the car to a corner space one storey below ground level.

He checked the contents of O'Cassidy's pockets. There was nothing in either of his trouser pockets except the torn half of a cinema ticket. The Irishman had seen a film entitled *Forty Pounds of Trouble*, starring Tony Curtis, in a cinema somewhere in Surrey the night before. Vernon had seen the film in London recently, and thought the Irishman's choice of an evening's entertainment was rather childish.

In O'Cassidy's right inside jacket pocket, was a photograph, presumably of the woman whom he had referred to as his "beloved Mary." She was not particularly pretty, but she had large, kindly blue eyes and a radiant smile. Her fresh, innocent face was framed by a shock of red curls. Vernon felt a lump in the back of his throat, and put the photograph away.

The jacket's left hand pocket contained an Irish passport, bearing the name Finbar Brendon Patrick O'Cassidy. His date of birth was quoted as being 16th March, 1928. Vernon made a mental note of the date and forced himself to learn it by heart, in case questioned, even over a minor driving offence.

The address given was Manor Bralee, Borris-in-Ossory, County Laois, Eire. This information corresponded with the name, date of birth and address on the driving licence, tucked neatly inside the passport. The wallet, which Vernon had stolen, contained twenty pounds.

The glove compartment contained a map of England and Ireland, which Vernon would need when travelling to the port of Fishguard in Pembrokeshire, before boarding the ferry for Rosslare. He said, half to himself and half out loud, "I'm bored stiff and sick to death of the sight of blood. Four's enough for me. There won't be five."

Vernon was satisfied with the excellent progress he had made since leaving Farnham. He locked all four doors of the Rover, including the boot, which contained O'Cassidy's suitcase as well as his own luggage. He desperately needed somewhere to rest for two hours, and decided there would be no better place for this purpose, than the front row of the crowded public gallery at the Old Bailey. It was there that Stephen Ward, about whom he knew nothing whatever, would be giving his evidence.

He went to the front of the queue where he saw two shady-looking men with Brylcreemed black hair and sunglasses.

"What are you up to?" one of the men said

suspiciously.

"Are you selling seats?" asked Vernon in the soft Irish accent he had decided to adopt, which he found easier than an American accent.

"Yes," said one of the men. "Give me twenty-five pounds and I'll disappear. You'll be the first to get in to hear the filthy old ponce."

Vernon handed over twenty-five pounds in five pound notes and put his wallet back in his pocket.

"Thanks, governor," said the man. "That'll keep me going. I'm off down the greyhounds."

A woman, who had queued all night, but without standing a chance of attending the hearing, was leaning against the wall, exhausted and incensed.

"You can't go paying your way to the head of the queue, you bastard!" she shouted.

Vernon was relieved not to have to speak. The woman standing behind him interjected.

"Mind your own business. Anyone who pays for something's got the right to have it."

Vernon noticed that the woman supporting him was about twenty and wearing an ill-fitting red wig. Two places behind her, stood a woman aged about fifty, wearing an equally ill-fitting blonde wig. A third woman, in her early seventies, was leaning exhaustedly on her walking stick, with her head turned self-consciously towards the wall, wearing a black wig.

Although Vernon had an infuriating tendency to be absent-minded and thoughtless, he was observant enough to notice that these three women were wearing wigs. He also realized that they were related, due to their similar facial features, despite their difference in age. All three had aquiline noses, high cheekbones and almond-shaped, melancholy, eyes.

He concluded that the woman, who spoke up for him, was the daughter, and that the other two were her mother and grandmother. Each appeared to be hiding her face from the other, as if ashamed to be seeking such insalubrious entertainment.

A policeman opened the heavy oak door leading to the court at 9.45. The three women still avoided eye contact with each other, and ran frantically up and down on the spot. They were terrified of being overtaken by faster runners in the queue, and deprived of seats in the front row of the public gallery. This could only be reached by racing, with manic desperation, up four flights of stairs, each step heavily dented by stampeding ghouls over decades.

The policeman, who opened the door, was familiar with the frenzy of the hoards. He stood with his arms on each side of the door, looking hassled, apprehensive and bored. He had bitter memories of the crowd who had trampled over him, knocking him flat on his back, when Mandy Rice-Davies was due to give evidence.

"Don't panic! Don't panic!" he screamed, ignorant of the fact that he himself was panicking within, even more than the crowd.

Vernon was fitter than the people behind him, and walked up the stairs, taking three steps at a time, easily outpacing those trying to overtake him. The three women were all fast runners and caught up with him, each glaring at the other, for having the effrontery to be interested in such a "sordid" matter. They were too tired to notice each other's presence in the queue, despite the twenty-year-old's outburst, and were furious that their disguises had been recognized.

Vernon was the first to enter the public gallery, and sat quietly at the far end of the front row, with the best view of the witness box. Next to him, sat the daughter of the bizarre trio. He felt endeared to her for protecting him from getting into a fight and making himself conspicuous. The crowd would have lunged towards him, had she not spoken up, and deprived him of his place in the queue.

A girl in her teens sat between Vernon's young benefactor and her mother. Two men sat between her mother and grandmother.

Vernon smiled at the daughter, who was so

lively and vivacious that he regretted his smile. She dug him sharply in the ribs.

"We've been found out, blast it!" she said in a hoarse whisper.

"Who was found out?" asked Vernon.

"We'd been queuing for two nights, bringing our flasks and sandwiches. You're not going to believe this. I came wearing a red wig, so as not to be recognized by my mother. My mother came in a blonde wig so that my grandmother wouldn't see her, and my grandmother put on a black wig so as not to be recognised by either my mother or myself.

"After all that, we all recognized each other. Our efforts were in vain. There's going to be a terrific row when we get home. It's not fair when you try hard without succeeding, is it, sir?"

Vernon was half asleep and disinterested in this tedious, unsolicited information.

"Sure, it's not," he muttered, only just remembering his Irish accent.

The young woman had a strange penchant for bald-headed men, and hoped to befriend him on a long-term basis.

"Where are you from?" she asked.

"Southern Ireland."

"Where in Southern Ireland."

"Oh, the country. I live near Borris-in-Ossory."

"That's a funny name. I suppose you're in

London on holiday?"

"Yes, said Vernon, leaning over the gallery rail with his eyes shut."

The woman dug him excitedly in the ribs.

"Were you up here when Christine was giving her evidence?"

Vernon was already asleep.

"Were you up here when Christine was giving her evidence?" she repeated.

Vernon was becoming quite irritable. He couldn't stand being questioned, particularly when jolted from sleep.

"Christine who?" he asked abruptly, his soft Irish accent becoming unpleasantly harsh.

The woman looked at him aghast. He wondered whether she had seen his picture in a newspaper, and had somehow recognized him under his immaculate disguise. He broke out in a cold sweat.

The woman leaned over the teenager on her other side. Now that she knew that her mother was aware of her deceit, she pushed the teenager forwards and gripped her mother by the arm.

"What do you want, you dirty-minded young hussy?" said the mother.

"You won't believe this. Guess what the man said?"

"If it's filthy, I don't want to hear it, do I, dear?"

"It isn't. I asked the man ..."

"What man, dear?"

"The man next to me, o course. We got talking, and do you know he doesn't know who Christine is?"

"Oh, I do wish you'd keep your voice down," said the mother, "Don't you realize how embarrassed Grandma is, because you and I recognized her? Besides, the man next to you is an Irishman, unfamiliar with the names of witnesses in the case."

"Even so, it's extraordinary that he doesn't know who Christine is!" said the daughter in a shrill, piping voice.

The mother leant over to her daughter and grabbed her by the ear, hissing,

"Button your lip, babe, or you'll be sorry once we get outside!"

The daughter woke Vernon, yet again. He was averse to attracting further attention to himself, so he made up his mind to be as courteous as possible.

"I've got something really funny, to tell you," she began.

"Is that so, now?"

"I've got these two brothers. They couldn't come today because they're at work. You should have heard what happened at breakfast on Sunday. Like all of us, they're rivetted by this case, and they fought like animals for *The News of the World* which gives it the best coverage, and, of course, the best photographs of Christine. They both seized the newspaper, and tore it in half. One of them grabbed hold of a carving knife, and chased the other round the table. When I came down to breakfast, there was blood in the butter!"

Vernon was amused and had a giggling fit.

"To be sure, I come from an argumentative family," he said, "but I've never come down to breakfast and found blood in the butter. Blood in the butter, indeed, blood in the butter. Sure, that story's made my day!"

They were interrupted. The Judge entered the Court. Everyone in the room, including the occupants of the public gallery, rose. Ward walked to the witness box.

Vernon looked closely at Ward, and was intrigued by O'Cassidy's and the crowd's fascination for him. He remembered some mention of immoral earnings, and had overheard mutterings among the crowd outside the court, that there was a sordid element in Ward's character.

Vernon studied his face, and was struck by the extreme nobility of his features. Ward suddenly turned his head to one side, showing his profile. Vernon observed his nose, which was aquiline and infinitely larger than normal, like a gigantic, craggy rockface. Although Vernon did not consider him a handsome man, he felt, for some inexplicable reason, that his nose made him look even more distinguished than he appeared from the front.

He was deeply confused by references to his sordidness, when he heard him answering his cross-examining barrister's questions. He was struck by his aristocratic accent, and educated, articulate speech, but he failed to understand what he was talking about. He remembered the shady seat-salesman's description of him as a "filthy old ponce," and felt this expression was grossly at variance with Ward, who, to him, bore the grace and dignity of an anointed king.

Vernon's concentration, at the best of times, was poor, and on this occasion, was even worse. He soon lost interest in Ward's cross-examination, and slept until the end of the hearing. As he returned to O'Cassidy's car, he walked past a litter bin and pulled out a discarded copy of the most recent edition of the *Evening Standard*. Two thirds of the front page covered the court case. A small section at the bottom of the page read,

"Three dead bodies were found in a bedroom at the Hogg's Back Hotel in Farnham, Surrey.

"A blonde woman in her early twenties was lying dead on top of a man who was also dead.

A third person, a man known to be a nuisance and a homosexual, was lying on top of the bed face-downwards with a Smith and Wesson in his hand. There was a bullet wound in the back of his neck. Police are convinced his death was not suicide, but that a fourth person was involved, and that this person had been hired as a hitman to kill the dead woman's lover. Police are looking for a man, calling himself Paul Jones, who left the hotel during the night."

There was a small drawing of the suspect next to the article. Vernon was satisfied that it bore no resemblance to his present appearance. He felt calmer once he had reached the car. He studied the map and planned his awesomely long journey to Fishguard and across the Irish Sea to Rosslare. He knew he would find complete safety, and would be able to lie down on the back seat of the car, and sleep during the crossing.

Olive, Kelvin and Alan, also read the *Evening Standard*, which they bought every day since they had sent Eddy Vernon to the hotel. They passed the newspaper to each other in silence, broken by Kelvin.

"I knew all along the bastard would snarl things up!" he shouted. "He was only told to kill

Earnshaw. So what does he do? He kills Bamber's bloody wife as well, together with another man in the room. God, he's stupid!"

"Do you think he may have harmed himself as well?" asked Olive, anxiously.

"Nah, Mother. He's hiding somewhere. If his half-wittedness is anything to go by, he's probably gone back to the hotel and locked himself in his room! I'd give anything to see the face of the first member of hotel staff, witnessing this sea of dead bodies. I'd also like to hear the interpretations of the police, once called to the hotel."

The Hogg's Back cleaner arrived earlier than usual, on the morning Vernon had left. She was surprised not to find Vernon in his room, as she knew he liked to sleep late. The concierge had already told her that Chandler's mother was gravely ill, and that he had gone to see her before her death. She cleaned Vernon's room but avoided Chandler's room as she had done it the day before.

She had arrived earlier that day, because she had met a man who offered to take her swimming later that morning. He was attractive and she was determined not to let him down. They had arranged to meet at his house and he had urged her to finish her work as soon as she could.

She was overjoyed when she realized that the

only room left to clean was 309, with the devoted couple in it. She unlocked the door and opened it, singing an Elvis Presley song called *Wooden Heart*.

She soon stopped singing when she saw Earnshaw's, Sally's and Chandler's bodies on the bed. She fainted and when she came round, she noticed that Sally and Earnshaw had been murdered first.

As the gun was in Chandler's hand, she assumed the murders had been part of a triangular suicide pact. It didn't occur to her that Chandler's fatal wound had been fired through the back of his neck, disproving that he had inflicted it himself.

She was bitterly disappointed not to be able to keep her swimming appointment with her attractive new friend. Once she had reported the murders to the concierge, he would call the police and she would have to describe at length what she had seen.

The concierge was mortified by the fact that three murders had taken place in the hotel he had been put in charge of, while his senior colleague was on leave. He was also afraid that his superior might sack him.

There was no way in which he could remove the bodies, once the cleaner had found out about them, so there was little alternative for him but to call the police. He re-read the interminable, bizarre, semi-humorous letter which "Paul Jones" had left on his desk earlier that morning, and decided to show it to the police when they arrived.

The police turned up within ten minutes, screeching their panda car to a halt in the hotel drive. They came into the lobby. There were two of them, Detective Inspector Rattery and Detective Constable Rush.

Rattery was a formidable-looking man. He was tall and robustly built, and had an exceptionally rude manner. Rush looked like a dwarf beside him. He was unfit and was short and stout. He was a sad-looking man because he knew he looked ridiculous.

The police, the concierge, the porter and the disappointed cleaner, all stood up while discussing the murders. The cleaner described what she had seen in room 309, and also told the two officers exactly what she had reported to the concierge.

The concierge had little to add, other than the act of showing "Paul Jones's" letter to Rattery and Rush in turn. They were amused and baffled by the letter, and were deeply suspicious of its author, whom they assumed probably suffered from some form of mental disorder.

"All right," said Rattery, "my colleague and I will inspect room 309, and try to find out whoever else was involved. You very kindly gave us the names of the murdered man and woman, as well as the homosexual. One of the things we will investigate will be whether or not those are their real names. Would you mind giving me the key to that room, sir?"

Rattery found the room worse than he expected. "Good God, what a dreadful smell! I'm surprised that concierge didn't issue us with an airspray."

"It would have helped," said Rush timidly.

"I can't stomach this hole", said Rattery, "Go and make an examination while I stand by the door."

Rush went closer to the bodies. "Yes, sir. It's clear the man and woman were lovers."

"That's obviously so. You'll have to come up with something a bit sharper than that."

"It looks as if someone opened the skylight, sir. The blonde woman couldn't have been shot at close range. As for the man under her, the killer must have climbed into the room and shot him. His natural reaction was to turn his head away from the killer, which is why he was shot in the back of the head. I've no idea what the motive for killing them both was, sir."

"Don't be daft," barked Rattery. "It looks as if the woman's husband hired a hitman to kill them. Rigor set in yet, Rush?"

Rush touched the couple's limbs and found them stiff. "Yes, sir, they're both in rigor, all right. Stiff as a couple of boards. Would you like to come over and check?"

"Certainly bloody not, you fool! Take a look at the man in the pink suit, sprawled on top of them."

"First, he was sick before the bullet entered his neck," ventured Rush.

"Yes, yes, I can smell it. God, this is unpleasant!"

"He was shot in the back of the neck," said Rush, "and the bullet exited on the other side. Like the man in bed on his back, he, too, was shot at close range. I think he was the hitman. He couldn't take the strain, so he shot himself in the back of the neck. Suicide."

"Can you imagine someone committing suicide via the back of their neck?" asked Rattery.

"Well, it's been done in this instance, sir."

"You really are a daft man, Rush."

"If it wasn't suicide, what was the Smith and Wesson doing in his hand?" said Rush.

"Can't you work it out? A fourth man, presumably calling himself Paul Jones, came into the room via the skylight and shot the man. He must have lost his head. He meant to make it look like suicide, which is why the Smith and Wesson was put into the dead man's hand. The only mistake he made was to shoot the man in the back of the neck.

"I would imagine two hitmen were involved. The concierge said the man in the pink suit's name was Tony Chandler. He said, that, while staying here, his mother was seriously ill and died. Apparently, he had tried to commit suicide by hanging himself on the pipe leading to his lavatory cistern.

"He didn't have much of a brain. The pipe broke and caused a flood. The hotel porter threatened to call the police because it was found out that he was a homosexual. The man calling himself Paul Jones must have feared this would thwart his plan to kill the two lovers, so he bribed the porter with ten shillings to keep his mouth shut.

"In his mad, dotty letter to the concierge, Jones said Chandler came into his room after midnight, brandishing a revolver. He said his mother had just died. What do you think happened then, Rush?"

"Chandler must have brought the revolver with him for one of two reasons. Either, he decided to kill himself because his mother had died. Or, he took it upon himself to climb through the skylight into this room, and kill the two lovers, as instructed."

"Do you think a man would wish to kill himself because his mother had just died?"

"Most men wouldn't," said Rush. "The concierge said Chandler was not only a nuisance, but also very unstable. It's possible his grief was such that he couldn't hold on any more."

"Why would he have come into this room to do it?" said Rattery.

"I don't know, sir. Perhaps he didn't kill himself. Perhaps he came here to do his job. Once he realized what he had to do, he couldn't face it, and was sick. Jones, who was likely to have been the second hitman, came here to see whether he had done the job correctly. He must have realized his accomplice was totally incompetent, and might spill the beans, so he killed him."

"That's one of your more intelligent interpretations of events, Rush. In his mad letter, which the concierge showed to us, surely you'll remember that he made no mention of his committing murder. What he did was quite clever. He complained that he had heard shooting in the street, as well as the sound of a car backfiring. He also said the noise had been so awful, that he demanded a refund of fifteen pounds for the time spent in this hotel. Do you remember him mentioning the Sun Inn in Weymouth?"

"Of course I do, sir."

"I'm convinced he shot Chandler, but even so, I want a patrol car in Weymouth, to check the Sun Inn, and find out whether Paul Jones is staying there. I bloody well hope he isn't because it would mean investigations about whoever killed Chandler, more complicated than they are, already.

"Just one other thing, Rush, go and see whether Chandler's in rigor, so that we can find out how much time elapsed after the killing of the two lovers. If he wasn't in rigor, it would mean that there had been some time between the first two murders and his murder. I hope to God that's not the case, as one thing I can't tolerate is an incomprehensible investigation."

Rush was exhausted, as well as confused by Rattery's monologue. He stood still, peering at Chandler's body, with his head bowed.

"Jesus, Rush, is there something wrong with your hearing? Check the stupid, little queer, and tell me whether he's in bloody rigor!"

Rush's self confidence always diminished when Rattery was rude and dismissive towards him. He made a superhuman effort not to burst into tears. He touched Chandler's right hand, which held the gun, and found that the hand was tightly clenched. When he tried to pull the fingers away, it seemed they were glued to the gun.

"Well, Rush, is it rigor, or isn't it?" shouted Rattery.

"Yes, sir. It's rigor *à la carte*."

"Don't be so damned silly!"

"Sorry, sir. In a case as bad as this, we need a

little black humour."

"That wasn't funny. It was stupid. If you really wanted to be funny, I'm sure you could have done better than that.

"There's another thing. The couple gave their names as Mr and Mrs Cyril Craddock when they checked in. Go through the jacket on the floor. Find out if these are their correct names. Also, I want you to find the girl's handbag, and check her identity."

Rush looked through the drawers, his hands shaking through fear of his boss.

"Come on, Rush! Do you know of any woman who keeps her handbag in a drawer? Try the cupboard."

Rush opened the cupboard and found a new-looking, black crocodile handbag, big enough to hold three thick books. Rush rummaged through the many items as quickly as he could. He found Sally's passport, opened it and read the name, Sally Julia Bamber.

He then picked up Earnshaw's jacket and found his driving licence in the inside pocket. The name given was Lt. Kenneth Francis Benjamin Earnshaw.

"Well?" asked Rattery.

"They registered under a false name," said Rush. "Their real names were Lt. Kenneth Francis Benjamin Earnshaw and Sally Julia Bamber."

"As I thought," said Rattery. "Now check the queer. He registered as Anthony Cecil Chandler. Roll him on his back, check his identity in his inside pocket, and then roll him back on his stomach."

Rush did as he was told. He found Chandler's driving licence in his inside pocket. The name given was the same as the name he had registered under.

"It's the same name, sir, Anthony Cecil Chandler."

"Good," said Rattery. "The next thing we'll have to do is find this man calling himself Paul Jones."

When the two officers left the hotel, they found a posse of newspaper reporters and photographers waiting for them. They said "no comment" to the reporters who took their photographs.

The gentlemen of the press were persistent. They waited for Rattery and Rush to leave, and went straight into the hotel. The young concierge was low in spirits and craved some excitement. He told them everything he knew, including the names of the three victims.

Claude Bamber never had time to read newspapers. He hadn't yet found out about the murders in the Hogg's Back Hotel, nor was he aware of the fact that Earnshaw was dead.

It was a hot morning, and he had been able to get a seat on the train to London for the first time for months. The man sitting opposite him, was looking at the back page of *The Daily Express*. Bamber was unable to miss seeing the front page headline in letters two inches high.

"Mass murder in Hogg's Back Hotel in Farnham."

He leant forward and read on.

"Three bodies were found in a bedroom in the Hogg's Back Hotel, Farnham, Surrey. It has been confirmed that one of the dead was Lt. Kenneth Francis Benjamin Earnshaw, who was found lying under the body of Sally Julia Bamber. Also, in the room, was the body of a certain Anthony Cecil Chandler, known to be a highly unstable homosexual. Police are looking for a man using the false name of 'Paul Jones'."

Against his name, was a picture of a man with thick black hair and sideburns.

It took Bamber five minutes to register that his wife had been murdered. He undid the top buttons of his shirt and loosened his tie and started to hyperventilate. He then took deep breaths and went out into the corridor to find Campbell, whom he knew would be standing in his customary place, looking out of the window.

Campbell was standing in the place where

Vernon expected to find him. He, too, was not a newspaper reader, and knew nothing about the fact that Bamber's wife was dead.

Bamber charged up to him and grabbed him by the collar.

"Whatever's the matter, Claude?"

"Look, you Scottish bastard, don't you dare ever call me by my first name again!"

"What's up? What have I done?"

"I'll tell you what you've done. I told you to tell your contacts in London, to see to it that only Lt. Earnshaw was killed. You've betrayed me, you stinking kilted traitor! You had my wife killed as well. Sally's dead, do you understand? She's dead, and you're responsible."

"I don't know what you mean," said Campbell. "I told them only to kill Earnshaw."

"If you told them that, why was my wife killed as well?"

"It really is nothing to do with me, Mr Bamber. I gave them your instructions, and the hitman they set up, must have bungled it."

"You lie! You lie! You lie! You lie!" screamed Bamber. "The proof is on the front page of *The Daily Express*."

"I never read *The Daily Express*!" bleated Campbell.

"You don't deserve to live, Campbell!" shouted

Bamber, as he grabbed him by the collar a second time and dragged him to the nearest door. Campbell was so frightened that he froze. Bamber threw the door wide open, and before his opponent could stop him, he pushed him through it with all the strength he could muster.

He shoved the man, whom he believed to have betrayed him, down a long, steep, cliff-like slope. The train moved so fast that he could not see the outcome of his action, but he was convinced that Campbell had fallen to his death. He had no idea that he had been seen, and that the police would be waiting for him at Waterloo Station.

Olive, Kelvin and Alan Vernon were having breakfast in their kitchen one Monday morning. Kelvin was drinking tea out of a saucer, ignoring the black looks his mother was giving him.

"Kelvin! Your manners are nothing short of vile. Pour the contents of your saucer into your cup and drink your tea from there. You really are an absolute barbarian."

"I'm sorry, Mother. I didn't sleep last night and I didn't think what I was doing."

"A likely tale! Why does it always have to be you who has filthy table manners, and not the others?"

"I did say I was sorry, Mother. I didn't do it on

purpose. Honest, I didn't."

Olive said no more. She spread butter and jam onto her bread, and drank her tea.

The family rose from the table. The telephone rang. It was one of those primitive telephones attached to the wall.

Kelvin answered it.

"May I speak to Mrs Olive Vernon, please?"

"Oh, that's my mother. Hold on a minute."

"Who was it, Kelvin?" asked Olive.

"I don't know, Mother."

"In that case, you should have asked, shouldn't you?"

"Yes, I should. I'm sorry."

Olive took the receiver from Kelvin's hand.

"Who is it?" asked Olive.

"I'm sorry to disturb you. This is the police station at St Paul's, London. I'm afraid you must prepare yourself for some very tragic news."

Olive knew that the news related to her youngest son. She felt a twingeing pain radiating across her top jaw. She began to sweat and breathe heavily and felt a painful cramp in her stomach. She pulled a chair towards the telephone, and sat on it, her face white.

Kelvin came up to her and held her hand.

"What's the matter, Mother?"

She waved him away and pressed the receiver to

her ear.

"What's happened?" she asked.

"It's about your son, Edmund. His body has been found in an underground carpark in West Smithfield, London, EC4, near the meat market. It would seem he'd taken his life. His throat's been slit from ear to ear with a razor blade, which was found on the concrete. Our officers have gone through his pockets, and found plenty of evidence of his identification, as well as your name and telephone number. His body is in the mortuary at St Bartholomew's hospital."

Olive let out a horrifying wail and fell off her chair in a faint. Kelvin brought her round by patting her face with cold water. He lifted her back onto the chair and held her hand, while Alan made her some tea.

"Is it about Eddy, Mother?" asked Kelvin.

"Yes. He's dead. His body was found in the Smithfield underground carpark. He'd slit his throat. The police said his body's in St Bartholomew's Mortuary."

"I'll go and identify the body," said Kelvin. "I've been to that hospital before. I know how to get there."

"Before you go, will you help me up to bed?"

"Of course, Mother. Can Alan or I bring you anything?"

"Yes. Brandy."

"I'll help you up. Then I'll bring some to your room. You'll feel better after it."

"Thank you so much, Kelvin, my son."

Eddy's loss did not effect Kelvin, but because his mother meant so much to him, he was saddened for her sake, and did not like the idea of going to a mortuary.

He took an amphetamine to raise his spirits, and once in good humour, he took the underground train to St Paul's, the closest station to the hospital. His spirits had risen even higher, as he walked to the hospital. He broke from a walk into a run.

He noticed the high graffiti on the wall to the left of the main gate which puzzled him.

THIS HOSPITAL IS AS CORRUPT AS CALIGULA'S ROME.

He wondered what this meant and was particularly confused as he had no idea who Caligula was. He walked straight into the hospital. A festival known as "View Day", was taking place, an occasion which usually took place much earlier in the summer, but for some unknown reason, it was later this year.

He was intrigued by the stalls which sold T-shirts, with the hospital's name on them, books describing its history, and a stall selling postcards, showing the place as it was a hundred years ago.

Other stalls sold cakes, buns and chocolates. Kelvin felt hungry and bought cakes and buns which he crammed into his mouth.

He saw men in striped trousers and long black coats. He did not know that these men, gathered in groups, stuffing cake into their mouths, were consultants, men at the top of the medical ladder.

He turned round to look at the grey stone architecture behind him. He saw a man, aged about fifty, obviously keen on the music of the late fifties and early sixties, coming through the main gate. The man was smiling inanely, and making exaggerated rock 'n' roll movements. His name and rank were printed on his lapel. He was Michael Rookwood, the Senior Hospital Administrator. He was known as the "Rocker" because he was unable to control his movements, particularly when he was nervous.

He rocked all the way to the cake-eating consultants. Kelvin stood near them, intrigued by what the Rocker was about to say. He spoke with a heavy Yorkshire accent, and never used the definite article.

"Gentlemen, this is a highly important matter," he began. "Are you able to attend a Board Meeting tomorrow morning?"

"What's all this in aid of, Michael? I do wish you'd stand still," said one of the consultants.

"Very very urgent," said the Rocker, breaking nervously into rock 'n' roll movements, once more. "What time suits you all?"

The consultants muttered among themselves. Some of them said their Senior Registrars could stand in for them at their clinics. They agreed that 11.00 o'clock would be a convenient time.

"Would you mind telling me what this Board Meeting is about?" asked another consultant.

The Rocker raised his voice because his nervousness had increased. His rock 'n' roll movements had become even more pronounced, as did his heavy Yorkshire accent, devoid of the definite article.

"There's an awful lot of necrophilia going on in mortuary!" he shouted. "I know its bloomin' rude, but it's a soobject that's got to be addressed!"

"Could you please tell me where the mortuary is?" asked Kelvin. "I've got to identify my brother."

The Rocker continued to rock.

"Sorry about that, sir. Just turn round, facing gate. Before you get to gate, turn left and go down steps and ring bell."

Kelvin followed the simple instructions. He went down the steps and rang the bell. The amphetamine had made him even more high-spirited, and he had a giggling fit, brought on by the Rocker's extraordinary speech mode. The door was opened by a mortuary attendant who was a temporary, with a strident, upper class accent.

"Who are you, and what are you laughing at?" he asked.

"I've just heard the funniest thing in the world. The Administrator, a Yorkshireman, never says 'the'," said Kelvin.

"That must be Mike Rookwood," muttered the attendant. "What did he say?"

"He said,

"'There's an awful lot of necrophilia going on in mortuary. I know it's bloomin' rude but it's a soobject that's got to be addressed.'" Kelvin did an exaggerated imitation of the Rocker's Yorkshire accent, and added, "Whenever the man walks, he rolls about like a ball."

The mortuary attendant had, himself, indulged in the practice the Rocker had condemned. This did not deter him from being angry and pompous. He showed exaggerated, xenophobic arrogance, typical of most who work with the dead.

"Mortuaries!" he shouted with a loud, public school accent, "are places to be spoken about with fucking reverence! Incidentally, what are you doing here?"

"My name's Kelvin Vernon, and I've come to identify the body of my brother, Edmund

John Vernon."

"Oh. I'm sorry. Let's have a look."

The attendant scoured what looked like several rows of rugger-players' lockers. The room smelt of unwashed socks and formaldehyde. The walls and floor of the room, were unwashed. To make the place even more unpleasant, the names of the deceased were chalked onto the drawers, when it would have looked nicer, had they been typed, put in cellophane covers, and neatly pasted on.

The attendant found the drawer containing what he thought were the remains of Edmund John Vernon. He pulled it out gently.

"There we are, sir. Would you like me to put on an overhead light, so that you can see better?"

"No thanks. I can see all right. Would you let me stay here alone for a few minutes, so that I can think of my brother?"

"Certainly, sir. No problem at all."

Kelvin knew immediately that the body pulled out on the sliding drawer, was definitely not his brother's. The bald head could have been seen as an attempt at disguise, but nothing else showed that the body belonged to Eddy Vernon.

Kelvin opened the corpse's eyes and found they were smallish and bright blue. Eddy's eyes were large and brown. He remembered Eddy's nose, which was strong and straight and noticed that the man in the drawer, had a long, pointed nose. Even Eddy's ear lobes were different from the man's. He had thin ear lobes, and the ear lobes on the dead body were thick.

Kelvin knew that it would not be advantageous to him or his family, to tell the mortuary attendant that the body was not his brother's. Police interrogators would come to the house on a daily basis, and each member of the family would be cross-examined. While these thoughts were passing through his head, he decided to tell the attendant that his brother was indeed dead and that the body he had come to identify, was his.

"Are you ready, yet, sir?" asked the attendant.

"Yes. I'm afraid he was my brother. The facial features, and the contents of his pockets, are his. I'll arrange his funeral. My poor mother is mortified."

Kelvin left the mortuary, turned left at the top of the steps, and exited the hospital through the main gates. He turned left, again, and went into a public call box, its walls peppered with the names of prostitutes and their telephone numbers. He frenziedly rang his mother's number.

"Mother! Listen, I've got wonderful news!"

"What wonderful news?"

"I've been to the mortuary to identify Eddy.

I recognized everything, from the watch you gave him, the St Christopher medallion round his neck, and the contents of the pockets. You must know by now what he's done. He took another man into his trust, held him up at gunpoint, and made him take off his clothes which he put on, himself.

"As the man in Eddy's clothes, had nothing in his wallet, Eddy must have taken the lot. This is the only intelligent thing that boy's ever done in his life."

"So, he's not dead?" shouted Olive.

"No, of course not. He took over a man's identity and put his own clothes onto the man's body.

"When asked, I told the man on duty, that Eddy was dead. That will save the police looking all over the country for him. But it won't stop them asking us wacky questions such as, had we known he had suicidal tendencies. We must all say, we had no idea why the death could have taken place, but that he was behaving strangely weeks before."

Kelvin's coins began to run out.

"Put more in, quick," said Olive.

Kelvin got more coins from his pocket and dropped some of them on the floor.

"Just be grateful he's *not* dead. He's probably

fled the country. He'll be back with us, in not too long a time," said Kelvin.

"What do you think Eddy did with the man whose identity he took?"

"Don't be silly, Mother. There's a dead man in the mortuary. Eddy killed him, obviously."

"I'm so happy he's not dead. Shall we get together at The Sawdust tonight, and celebrate?"

"I don't see why not," said Kelvin. "Then I'll go down the knackers tomorrow, and arrange for his burial. Is there anything to identify the Hogg's Back murders with our family?"

"Nah!" said Olive. "The whole case is too confusing. Also, Eddy shaved his head, stole someone's identity, and went on the run."

Kelvin, Alan and Olive went to The Sawdust pub that evening. It was the first time they went to make merriment, rather than to discuss killing contracts. The Vernon boys, delirious that their once-grieving mother was joyful, ordered neat whisky. Kelvin had picked up the rock 'n' roll movements from the Rocker at the hospital, who had amused him so much by his failure to use the definite article.

He danced with his mother. She giggled drunkenly as he taught her to rock 'n' roll. Alan, too, was familiar with this mode of dancing, and he danced at length with his mother, until she was so drunk that she fell to the floor.

Eddy Vernon eventually reached the port of Fishguard, and as it was late at night, he had no difficulty getting a place on the ferry to Rosslare. He had planned to sleep in the back of O'Cassidy's Rover, but once he lay down, he felt strangely wide awake. The exceptionally long drive had given him a surge of energy.

Suddenly, he became inquisitive. He took O'Cassidy's suitcase from the boot, and as it was unlocked, he opened it and tipped its contents onto the passenger's seat.

He expected to find fairly conventional items in the suitcase, such as night clothes, a change of clothes, washing materials, possibly a book of Irish poetry, and even a Bible and perhaps a crucifix.

As he went through the contents of the suitcase of a man who had been so kind to him, he thought his tiredness had made him hallucinate. The first item he saw was a woman's white silk nightdress, violently torn in a few places and covered with bloodstains. The blood was not menstrual blood, as it appeared on the areas of the shoulders, chest and back.

He unrolled the nightdress and found a bloodstained cosh wrapped in it. He lit a cigarette and pulled hard on it as he looked at the other things in the suitcase.

There was a book by the Marquis de Sade entitled *Juliette, or the Prosperity of Vice*. He found copious references to flagellation, coprophilia, orgies and persistent sodomy in it. He was astounded by the fact that a seemingly gentle, kind man, should have carried such things in his suitcase.

There was another book entitled *Medical Jurisprudence and Toxicology*, which contained endless coloured photographs of children dying gruesome deaths. Vernon also found two paperback books about the perversions of the criminal mind, which could have been connected with his passionate wish to attend the trial of Stephen Ward.

He was about to close the suitcase, when he saw a piece of paper among the books. It was a letter from the woman her husband had referred to as his "beloved Mary".

He held it up towards the light, and read it, half to himself and half out loud.

"My dear Finni,
Although I have tried to live with you, I cannot. I have nowhere else to go so I am ending my life. By the time you read this, I will be dead. I will have taken a bottle of sleeping pills. When morning comes, my soul will have fled my body.
Had you been kinder to me, I would never have

done this, as it is a sin. Some days, you were so sweet, gentle and saintly, and I know that is how strangers see you. Other days, you knocked me about, dragged me out of bed at one o'clock in the morning when you came back drunk and hungry, wanting a meal.

You used a cosh on my body. You kicked me in the stomach, but as you were doing these things, you kept repeating how beloved I was to you, and how much it meant to you to keep my photograph with you at all times.

Goodbye, Finni, we'll meet in hell.
From your wife,
Mary."

Vernon fell asleep after reading what he considered to be a deeply disturbing letter. His sleep was broken by nightmares. He saw Alan and Kelvin walking round the cars on the ferry, with bloodstained coshes in their hands and murder in their hearts. He saw his furious mother looking for him so that she could flagellate him. Just behind her, was a dead child impaled on a spike.

One fortunate factor in his deep shame and guilt about murdering O'Cassidy, was his knowledge that he was not the seemingly saintly man he had met, but a monster. He felt better once the ferry arrived at Rosslare. He knew he was fundamentally weak and soft, unlike his brothers, so the events of the past few days, had traumatized him more than he could bear. He would have nothing to do in Ireland other than hide, rest and brood. It would be his inactivity, which would lead him to ruin.

He stopped the car intermittently on his way to Dublin, lay down on the back seat, and slept. He went to a country pub, expecting to find a choice of food, and whisky to wash it down with.

The pub was unlike any pub in London. What struck him first was the fact that there were no women present. Customers appeared to be drinking for the sake of drinking, without socializing. The place lacked the camaraderie and gaiety of a London pub. No conversations were taking place. A few men, the worse for wear, sprawled across chairs, snoring.

Vernon knew there would be nothing to eat. Like any murderer, he was suffering from inordinate gloom. He drank almost half a bottle of *Paddy's* whisky, which only a man is allowed to do in Ireland. He called the barmaid, a woman of about twenty-five, who looked fifty.

"Any hotels nearby?" he asked, remembering his Irish accent, even in his drunkenness.

"Patrick Pearse Inn, a mile to the left, on the left hand side," she said, without smiling.

By the time he reached the inn, he removed his

two cases but left O'Cassidy's behind in the boot. His drunkenness had reached a peak. He left the keys in the ignition and the doors unlocked.

He moved out of the small, bleak hotel the following day, after having several whiskies at the bar. He went into the tiny hotel carpark and found that O'Cassidy's car was missing. He didn't need to come to his senses to realize it had been stolen.

He staggered back to the hotel and went to the bar, where the barman was wary of him as he had been sick there earlier that morning.

"My car's been stolen," he told the barman.

"All you have to do is ring the Garda and give them the registration number."

"What are the Garda?" asked Vernon, inadvertently resuming his slight London East End brogue. The barman looked at him, startled.

"I thought you were Irish," he said.

"Yes, but I've spent a lot of time in England recently. Perhaps my accent confuses you. Would you mind telling me what the Garda are?"

The barman continued to polish wet glasses with an unwashed towel. He failed to look up.

"The Garda are the police," he said. "They're the people you tell — about the registration number of your car."

"I don't know the number of the car."

"I think you drink far too much to be driving a

car," said the barman.

Vernon eased his weight onto a bar stool and fell over. The barman raised his eyes to the ceiling.

"Any idea how I get transport to Dublin?" asked Vernon.

"There's a 'phone in the hall. Ask for a taxi to take you to the nearest railway station."

"What's the name of the station?"

"No idea. Are you going to be sick again?"

"No. I don't think so."

"You'd better not. My wife was on her knees clearing up after you, earlier. If you feel sick, go outside!"

"I think I can hold it."

"If there's any chance you can't, get yourself outside. I'll be happier when you've gone."

"In that case, will you call a taxi for me, to get rid of me?"

"Sure, I'll do that. It will be the making of my day."

The barman rang the only taxi company within an area of fifty miles. He let the 'phone ring for ten minutes and got no answer. Vernon leant back into an armchair. The barman was terrified he was going to be sick a second time.

"Sorry, sir, you'll have to go on foot," he said. "I'm not taking you in the van because of what could happen. A number of cars come down this road. You should get a lift soon enough."

"All right, I'll do that, but first, may I buy a bottle of *Paddy's* whisky?"

"As long as you don't drink it in this hotel. Go and stand outside the door. I'll bring it out to you."

Vernon paid for the whisky which he put in one of his cases. He started to walk down the narrow, deserted road. He drank more whisky to moderate his nausea. He waved at occasional passing cars. No-one would stop for him because of his staggering gait.

He wandered off the road, into a field and lay down in the long grass. The surreal events of the last few days, had finally robbed him of his sanity. His mind blocked out most of his short-term memory. He no longer knew of the murders he had committed. He knew that he had two violent, threatening brothers who were looking for him, intending to kill him.

He also knew that he had been involved in some obscure way with a man called Bamber. He tried to remember whether this were a person's name, or whether it were just a word which kept repeating itself in his head.

He heard a voice in rhythm to his pulsating temporal artery. He had no idea who he was or where he was. All he could hear was "Bamber bamber bamber bamber."

He took two more swigs, and without knowing where he was going or why, he went out into the road and knelt down, unaware that he was endangering himself. He repeated the name aloud which would not go away. He wondered whether he was hearing it, or whether it was a parasite eating into his brain. Bamber bamber bamber bamber.

A Garda patrol car came towards him. Two officers got out and helped him to his feet.

"That was silly and dangerous," said one. The second officer was more sympathetic. He put his hand on Vernon's shoulder.

"What is it, son?"

"I don't know who I am. Just that my brothers are following me. They want me dead."

"Why should they want you dead?"

"I don't know. I don't remember. I've forgotten who I am." He then wept and shouted hysterically, clutching the second officer's arm. "All I remember is this word, Bamber bamber bamber!"

"Perhaps, I can help you to find out what this means. Is it a person?"

"Bamber bamber bamber bamber!"

"Is it a word?"

"I don't even know that."

"Is it a horse you backed?"

"No."

"Is it something to do with your brothers?"

"I don't know. I know nothing. Bamber bamber bamber bamber!"

The two officers ushered Vernon into the patrol car and put his cases in the boot.

"Where are we?" shouted Vernon. "Where are you taking me?"

"At the moment, you are four and a half miles away from Dublin. We'll be taking you to the station. We want you to know that we won't hurt you. All we want to do is help you."

They got to the police station. Vernon sat down and went into a trance.

"If you empty your pockets, we can tell you who you are," said the more sympathetic Garda officer.

Vernon failed to raise his arm so the officer did so for him.

"Listen carefully, sir. Your name is Finbar Brendon Patrick O'Cassidy. You were born on 16th March, 1928. Your home address is Manor Bralee, Borris-in-Ossory, County Laois. Do you feel any better now we've told you your name?"

Vernon had still lost track of his memory. Even if he had been told his real name, he would not have reacted differently.

"You won't let my brothers in here, will you?" he said hysterically.

Two psychiatrists were sent for. They were both

kind to Vernon and assured him that he would soon have peace of mind.

He was transferred to an old asylum in Dublin. He still had plenty of money, but not enough to pay for his long-term incarceration. He was then sent to a pauper's asylum, also in Dublin, and was detained under Section 3 of the Irish equivalent of the Mental Health Act. This meant he would be confined to the pretty, cheerful gardens, with locked iron gates and walls too high for him to escape.

The only person he had contact with, was his regular psychiatrist. He did not befriend any of the nurses because they changed their shifts so often, and he was unable to tell one nurse from the other.

A kind-hearted hospital visitor came to see him three times a week. She was about sixty and was known as "Biddy".

Vernon told her of his loneliness and his adament refusal to make friends with any of the other patients.

He was Biddy's favourite, due to his large, cow-like eyes. She assumed, for some reason, that he was keen on sports. His boyish face and muscular figure were the main factors behind her conclusion.

One day, she bought him a box of golf balls for his use after leaving the asylum, but he was too doped to know what they were. He opened the box after her visit, and emptied it over his psychiatrist's head.

The doctors kept him asleep for a few days with the sedating drug, Chlorpromazine, in an attempt to resurrect his mind and sharpen his vision of reality. The staff were kind to him. They told him he could go out and sit in the garden if he wished.

The garden was on the same level as the medical secretaries' office. Sometimes, Vernon peered through the window and saw five secretaries sitting in a row, typing. He looked at each one in turn. The one sitting at the end of the row nearest to the window, had long black hair, swept back from her face, reaching her waist. Even in the distance, Vernon could see her bright emerald eyes which shone like diamonds, and noticed her resemblance to his mother.

Vernon looked through the window several times a day. He assumed all these girls were intelligent and well-qualified because of the nature of the work they were doing.

Occasionally, the office supervisor would come into the room. She had a strong English upper class accent, and a strident, bombastic manner. She was between fifty and sixty with a bitter, ageing face and dyed red hair.

Vernon could see that she was having a terrifying effect on the girls. He focused his eyes on the green-eyed beauty at the end of the row. He tried to attract her attention, but never did so when her British overseer was in the office.

One morning, he tapped on the window closest to her. He smiled wistfully, and felt it an advantage that his black hair had grown back; he had shaved the sideburns off.

She returned his smile. The following day, as his faculties were partially returning to him, he threw a note addressed to her through the open window. It read, "Yours is the most beautiful face I have ever seen. Will you come to the window one day, when the boss isn't here?"

She smiled and nodded her head. He was still confused, but her smile cheered and encouraged him.

Vernon backed away from the window, on seeing the British overseer coming into the office. A telephone was ringing on the desk of one of the other secretaries, so engrossed in her work that she didn't notice it.

"Answer that telephone, this instant, Sheila O'Reilly," commanded the Briton.

Sheila was plain. Her long, rusty blonde hair was scraped back from her face in a slide and she wore no make-up. She lifted the receiver, said "hullo" and identified the hospital. The caller was no longer on the line.

"What happened?" asked the overseer.

"The caller hung up, Miss," said Sheila.

"Didn't you hear it ring? Is there something wrong with your hearing?"

"No, Miss. I was trying to decipher my shorthand. I didn't notice it ring. It won't happen again."

"Kindly see that it doesn't. That is if you wish to stay here."

Vernon returned to the window. He was fascinated by all these women and their supervisor. He had never seen a collection of women before, as he had always lived and mixed among men.

The supervisor walked towards the black-haired woman for whom he held such a fascination. She was typing busily because the boss was in the office. The Briton tapped her on the shoulder.

"Marion McManus, have you been keeping the Suicide Book up to date?" she demanded in a barking, intimidating tone.

"Yes, Miss." Her Dublin accent was refined, unlike Sheila's. Vernon was rivetted by the two different Irish accents.

It was Marion who had been entrusted with the Suicide Book. Any occurrence of a suicide committed by a patient, both within, and outside the hospital, had to be noted in this long, thin, black book, and information had to be entered into columns, headed, Name, Age, Method of Suicide,

Motive for Suicide (if known), Date, Time and Place of Suicide.

"When was your last entry, Marion McManus?" asked the Briton accusingly.

Marion opened the book. "I have the details here, Miss. *The Dublin News* rang up at 9.17 this morning, asking for information. The body of a forty-year-old man, named as Patrick O'Flynn, recently discharged from this hospital, was dragged out of the Liffey between 4.00 and 4.30 this morning. His reason for suicide was the sudden departure of his wife, fifteen years his junior, according to the sodden note in his pocket. When he jumped from a bridge, some twenty feet above water level, he did not die on hitting the water. He drowned slowly and painfully. It was found that his lungs were brimming with mud."

The overseer was impressed by Marion's meticulous attention to detail. Vernon had heard the conversation and found the overseer's final reaction to the dismal incident, callous.

She threw back her head, facing Marion but appearing to address each woman in the office, as if making a public display of her efficiency.

"G-o-o-o-d!" she shouted, loudly enough for the patients in the garden to hear, and left the room as swiftly and as silently as she had entered it.

Vernon was taken off the Section, within a few

weeks which meant he could walk about in Dublin whenever he wished, but he was told to return by nightfall.

He tapped on the open window of the secretaries' office and threw in a note to Marion.

"I've been taken off the Section and am free to go outside. Do you know of a pub where we could meet at 6.00 this evening?"

She went back to her desk, tore a sheet of paper from her notebook and wrote on it in a forward, slanting hand, while Vernon waited agonizingly, fearing rejection. She handed him the note.

"I will meet you at 6.00. Go to The Harp and Shamrock in Murphy Street. If you don't know the way, go by taxi and if you have no money, I will pay the fare."

Vernon was overjoyed, and still in possession of plenty of stolen money. He took a bus to the city centre, where he bought two smart, inexpensive suits, one for winter, the other, for summer. He also bought a number of white cotton shirts and two ties.

He went back to the hospital at 4.00 in the afternoon, bathed, shaved and put on the summer suit, matching tie, and one of the white shirts. He brushed his freshly-grown black hair until it shone. He picked two red roses from the garden, to give to Marion, and hailed a taxi.

The Harp and Shamrock was a small pub, with pictures of race horses on its walls. Marion was sitting at the bar, drinking vodka and tomato juice. Had she not been known there, she would not have been served. In Ireland, women on their own, particularly in pubs, are not provided for and are shown the door.

Vernon got onto the vacant bar stool next to Marion, admiring her tight-fitting black silk dress.

"I hope you understand, I'm very nervous, taking out a beautiful woman like yourself. Would you mind my buying myself a drink before I say anything?"

Marion turned to face him, and fixed him with the beguiling smile, which she had given him when he watched her through the window.

"I can wait. It's all right," she said.

Vernon swallowed a double whisky and bought Marion another drink. He felt sufficiently at ease to speak, although it was she who broke the silence.

"I can tell you're shy. It's rather attractive. What's your name?"

"Finbar O'Cassidy. I know yours. It's Marion. Marion McManus. It's a lovely name."

"You think so? I don't like it but I've learnt to live with it. Where are you from, Finbar?"

"I'm from the country. I live near Borris-in-Ossory, County Laois."

"All your life?"

"Sure. All my life."

Marion drained her second double vodka and tomato juice. She turned to face him a second time, her eyes hostile.

"Why can't you tell me who you really are, instead of putting up this façade?" she said suddenly, startling him so much that he nearly fell off his stool.

"I don't understand what you mean, Marion."

Had she not smiled as she spoke Vernon would have walked out. Instead, he listene .

"Firstly, you're not Irish, as you vould have me believe, by putting on a bogus Irish accent. At first, I was fooled by you, but your drinking has given you away. I think you're British. You come from London, somewhere in the East End. I can tell by the lapsing of your vowels.

"Before you had your drink, your disguised accent was not all that obvious. Now, any fool can see through it. I'm no idiot. I can always tell when someone pretends to be what they're not. Also, I find it rather insulting to be thought stupid enough to believe a pack of lies.

"Suppose you tell me who you really are. Whatever the truth is, I won't tell anyone. You've my word on that, but if you go on lying, I will lose interest in you."

Vernon said nothing until he had bought another round of drinks.

"I'm sorry I lied, Marion. I'm afraid I'm not Irish. I'm British, and as you say, I do indeed come from London."

"Then stop speaking with this phoney Irish accent. Speak to me with your natural accent."

"I'll try. I've been in Ireland for a long time, so the accent comes naturally to me."

"Try harder."

Vernon was embarrassed and confused. When he used his natural accent, he kept lapsing into Irish vowels. She knew he was trying, and encouraged him by putting her hand on his.

"I'm in very serious trouble, Marion. That's how I got put in the asylum. I've got two vicious older brothers who are trying to find out where I am. That's why I came to Ireland. They want me dead."

"Why on earth should they want that?"

"They're both professional gangsters. They live on rackets. They live by violence and intimidation. They murder people and get paid for it. They extort money with menaces, and I wanted to break away from the family, altogether.

"That sort of life is not for me. All I want is a peaceful, straight life. They bullied me into murdering someone, and told me that if I didn't do what they told me to do, they'd do me in. I told them I'd do the job and I promised faithfully I would. I never did it, though. I got on a late night ferry and came here."

"Is it only your brothers who are after you, because you won't get involved with violence?"

"Yes. Well, there's my mother, too. She's very domineering and believes in crime. She controls my brothers."

"Do you love her?"

"I adore her, but I just don't want to be part of a family, committed to crime."

"You have a lot of money with you. Can I ask how you came by that?"

Vernon took another swig of whisky.

"I've been saving it up," he said, sounding as if he were telling the truth, "for years and years and years."

"How did you have it to save in the first place?"

"I'm afraid my mother gave it to me at regular intervals, on the proceeds of goods stolen by my brothers."

"So you have received money, knowing it had been stolen, but didn't steal any yourself."

"That's right."

"I know what you may be thinking," said Marion, "but I don't hold anything you say against you. Even if you'd confessed to being a practising contract killer, I wouldn't mind. All I care about is your telling me the truth about who you are and where you're from."

"Now that I've told you, how can you possibly be attracted to me?"

"You don't understand women," she said. "I like you because you bring out my maternal instinct. You are frail, vulnerable and dog-like. A woman is not interested in a man's past, but no woman will tolerate being lied to.

"There's another thing."

"What's that?"

"I like your British accent. There are different British accents, I know, but they all have in common that crisp, refreshing rasp."

"I don't understand you, Marion. It's a horrible accent. Why do you think I've tried to hide it?"

"It's not horrible. It's attractive. It's you. The next thing you can do, is tell me your real name. It's not Finbar O'Cassidy, and never was."

"I'll tell you, provided you'll always introduce me to others as Finbar O'Cassidy."

"Promise."

"Well, it's Eddy Vernon," he said with his head lowered, "but please keep that to yourself."

"All right. I will."

"It's just that I can't afford having my brothers catch up with me, and if they had any idea I was in

Ireland, they'd go from one city to another until they found me. Dublin is not a big place, and if someone has an English-sounding name like Vernon, word gets round fast. Anyway we've talked about me for long enough. Now, I want to hear your story."

"In the first place, I'm very rich," said Marion. "My father is a millionaire. He owns a chain of undertakers' offices in every city in Southern Ireland, and has branches in London and Manchester."

"And your mother?"

"She's dead."

"Sorry to hear that," said Vernon automatically, adding, "if you are rich, why do you go to work?"

"Because something tells me it's wrong not to work, even if I'm rich."

"Why? The only purpose of work is to live, and sometimes put a bit of extra by, to indulge in the occasional luxury. You can afford to do nothing all day."

"I'd feel really peculiar if I did."

"You get up early to arrive at 9.00 and you work through until 5.00."

"It comes naturally to me. That's the way I was brought up to live, to have continued constructive occupation."

Vernon had lost interest in her motives for

working. "What offices does your father work in?" he asked.

"The ones a mile up the road. They're very big. They're called P. S. McManus, Funeral Directors and Monumental Masons. He lives alone in a two-storey luxury flat above the shop. There's another, much smaller, tackier firm of funeral directors just a few yards down. They're all destructively jealous of my father's opulent offices.

"What makes the envy even worse is that their firm, who are known as Paddy O'Hara's Funerals, own just one hearse and two limos. My father's vehicles, on the other hand, cover a distance of at least thirty yards in the street. My father keeps two of his hearses in the garage at the back, and two more in the street, accompanied by his limos.

"So great is the animosity between Paddy O'Hara's Funerals towards my father's firm, that a member of their staff put an adhesive notice on the windscreen of one of my father's hearses, saying, 'Am Drunk. Will Remove Vehicle When Sober.'"

Vernon laughed spontaneously, but corrected himself when he noticed Marion was unamused.

"How unpleasant," he forced himself to remark.

"Yes. It was. It's certainly no laughing matter."

Vernon's pronounced shyness returned.

"Where do you live?" he asked.

"My father bought me a four-storey Queen Anne

house, half a mile away from the asylum."

"You live alone there?"

"Yes," she said assertively, adding, "But not tonight, I won't be. You'll be coming home with me. You don't have to live with me, only to spend tonight with me, and we'll see how we go from there."

"But Marion, I've never done this sort of thing before," he said. "I've no idea what to do."

"Don't worry. I'll teach you. By the time I've finished, you'll be the most accomplished lover in this city. You're going into that silly accent again, by the way, watch it."

"I'll have to use it when we're with other people so that my Englishness isn't noticed and talked about."

"All right, all right, but not when you're alone with me."

Marion drove Vernon back to the asylum the following morning just before 9.00. She returned to her desk as if nothing had happened. It had given her power and a sense of pleasure to give lessons in love-making to Vernon. To her, he was the replacement of a dog, on which she had once doted, but which had been run over.

Vernon was besotted by her, and spent the day reading James Hadley Chase outside the window, so that she could see the back of his head whenever she looked up from her work.

After two days, he moved into her house. He was humbled, at first, by its extreme grandeur and size and the priceless *objets d'art* it contained. She cooked for him each evening, and after dinner, they lay in bed, watching the television.

He continued to sit by the office window until the late Autumn when it became too cold, but he was content to pace up and down outside, as long as he could watch Marion working.

Three months had passed. They were dining, and Marion received an unexpected telephone call from her father, who was known simply as P.S. McManus.

"Hullo, Daddy. I haven't heard from you for a while. Are you well?"

"Yes. I'll come straight to the point." Vernon could hear his loud voice across the table. "It's come to my ears that you've got a man living with you. I've heard he's been there for quite some time."

"Why, yes, he has. How did you find out?"

"It doesn't matter how I found out. Out of elementary courtesy to me, it's time you brought him round to meet me. I suggest you bring him with you to lunch on Sunday."

"Is this an order?"

"Yes, it is an order. I've bought you a luxurious

house and a car to go with it. I can't think of any other fathers who lavish their daughters in this way. You haven't shown gratitude once. You're spoilt. I resent the fact that you've had a man living in your house, without telling me."

"Why should I have told you?" said Marion. "I'm over twenty-one. Besides, it isn't convenient for us to come this Sunday. We'll be out all day. We're driving to the country. We've been asked to lunch by one of my old school friends. After that, we're going to a museum. We can come the following Sunday, if you want."

"You will cancel the lunch!" snapped the father. "Even if you are over twenty-one, I still have the power to confiscate your house and car, if you refuse to do as I ask. I'm expecting you and your fancy fellow at 12.45 this Sunday. You're not living in a respectable, or decent manner. You're living in sin and I won't tolerate it."

"I must say, you are an awful bully."

"Perhaps I am. Either you come on Sunday, or you forfeit your house and car."

"All right. I don't have much choice, do I?"

The offices and residential quarters of P.S. McManus, Funeral Directors and Monumental Masons, were overbearing, ostentatious and indescribably vulgar. They had been designed by an

American architect hired by McManus.

The offices were on the ground floor. The front room was peppered with giant-sized Madonnas and Childs, their heads encircled by crude, glittering, gold halos. Each Madonna had tears on her cheeks, made of glass, which were illuminated by lights, turned on all day and all night.

Vernon found the general appearance of the place, threatening and frightening, and it increased his dread of meeting Marion's father.

"Come on. I know it's a bit overdone. The residential entrance is at the back of the building," she said.

She pushed a heavy, intricately-carved, gold bell into the wall with the palm of her hand. Two glossy black gates crashed open. The door to the lift was of 1930s American design. It reminded Vernon of the James Hadley Chase novel he had read when he was ill, set in 1930s America. Inside the lift, were elaborate black and gold carvings.

"My father will be on the second floor," said Marion in a stiff, nervous tone which increased Vernon's terror. They got into the lift which moved with a pronounced jolt. Vernon thought it was going to tumble into its shaft. He would have preferred it if it had, if only to save him from having to meet Marion's father.

The lift door opened automatically on the second

floor. A white-coated, bow-tied servant ushered them into an almost surreal room, its walls covered with mirrors, and its upright chairs made of glass.

"Welcome back, Miss Marion," said the servant. "Nice to see you after so long."

Marion took off her mink coat (a gift from her father) and handed it to the servant. "Thank you, Conlon," she said. "This is Mr O'Cassidy."

"Welcome to the premises, Mr O'Cassidy, sir. I'll have a word with you in private if I may." He beckoned Vernon into a corner.

"I have it in mind you're terrified of meeting Mr McManus," he began. "He has a daunting effect on strangers, I know, but his bark's worse than his bite."

"Just how bad is his bark?" ventured Vernon.

"Not quite as bad as they say."

"As who says?"

"Just visitors to the premises, that's all. He's coming into the room, now."

McManus was a tall, well-built man, aged about sixty, with handsome features, thick light brown hair streaked with grey and probing grey eyes. His voice, in harmony with his appearance, was carrying, and was garnished with a harsh Dublin accent, which daunted strangers and acquaintances alike.

He was holding half a glass of whisky in his

right hand. He wore a white linen suit, a pale blue shirt and an arresting red and black tie.

"Ah, Marion," he said, fixing his daughter with his penetrating stare.

"Hullo, Daddy. This is Finbar O'Cassidy."

Vernon offered his hand, but as his host was holding a glass, which he refused to transfer to his other hand, he failed to take it.

"I am most honoured to meet you, sir," said Vernon in a faltering whisper.

"Conlon, give this man a drink," said McManus. "As for you, O'Cassidy, go and sit on one of the glass chairs, and wait for me to come over."

Conlon brought Vernon some whisky which relaxed his nerves. McManus sat on another glass chair, so close to Vernon, it was almost touching him. Marion sat on a chair facing them. Despite the proximity between host and guest, McManus shouted throughout the conversation.

"There are two things wrong with you, O'Cassidy," said the host without preamble. "First, you're British. Second, you're drunk."

"I'm drunk because I'm very nervous, sir, but being British is no fault of mine."

"Why's your name O'Cassidy?"

"It was my father's name. I was brought up in London."

"You're familiar with my business, I take it? Do you know anything about funerals?"

"Funerals?"

"Yes, funerals. You must know what funerals are. They're those ceremonies which take place after we die."

"I don't know anything about them at all, sir," whispered Vernon.

"So, as I understand it, you know nothing about funeral direction?"

"No, sir." By now, the empty glass was shaking in Vernon's hand.

"Have you ever been to a funeral?"

"Yes. My father's."

"When did he die?"

"When I was quite young, sir."

McManus poured himself another drink, and put the decanter on the table.

"Burial or cremation?" he shouted.

"I beg your pardon, sir?"

"You're a slow man, O'Cassidy. Was he buried or cremated?"

"He was buried, sir."

"Sandalwood or pine?" bellowed the host.

Vernon felt as if he were going to be sick. "I'm sorry, but I don't understand your question, sir," he muttered.

"Oh, you're so deaf and slow! Was the coffin

Sandalwood or pine?"

"I don't know, sir."

"What living relations do you have? I'm thinking of Marion's security."

"A mother and two brothers, sir."

"And the professions of your brothers?"

"I don't know. I don't get on with them. I haven't seen them for some time. As far as I know, they're in London, sir."

"Why don't you get on with your brothers?"

"They've bullied me all my life."

"That's because you're a very weak man. You attract bullies. You are slow-witted and feeble," shouted the irascible host.

"Oh, please, Daddy," interjected Marion. "He's been ill. He's only just out of hospital."

McManus showed the first sign of enthusiasm during the conversation. He leant so close to Vernon that his terrified guest had to lean the other way.

"The only people in hospitals I'm interested in, are those I can send a man over to with a tape measure. Did you have anything which might recur, something nice and serious like cancer or a bad heart, that sort of brigade?"

"No, sir. I'm fully recovered."

"I don't think so. You've looked iller and iller since the time you sat down. I could still get my little man out to measure you up."

Marion mouthed to Vernon across the table.

"Psst! Daddy's making a joke. That means you've got to laugh."

"Ha, ha, ha!" Vernon was unamused, and the chuckle he gave was painful and forced.

"I'm talking seriously, now, O'Cassidy. I'm getting on and won't be around much longer. I need a replacement to ensure my Firm's stability in its Dublin offices. Marion, I think, is serious about you. Do you feel the same about her? I somehow don't think you're strong enough for her, do you?"

"I'll be the judge of that," said Marion, her voice raised.

"I am in love with your daughter, sir," said Vernon.

"As well you may be, but you're not intelligent and you're very timid."

"I am timid because you are intimidating me, sir," whispered Vernon.

McManus appeared to ignore the remark, but secretly respected Vernon's honesty.

"Are you prepared to take a course in funeral direction?" he asked, his voice still raised, as if his guest were sitting in another room.

"Yes, sir."

"Good. I'll book you into the Kevin Barry College of Funeral Direction and Embalmment. I can see you're quite a good-hearted young man, and you appear to be making Marion happy. It's true you haven't much of a brain and your reactions are very slow, but Marion has brought worse people than you over to see me. It's time we went into lunch."

The walls of the dining room were also covered with mirrors. No-one spoke during lunch, except McManus. Vernon was superstitious, and he had an irritating habit of throwing spilt salt over his left shoulder.

"Young man, will you kindly stop throwing salt all over the room! Who do you think's going to clear it up?" shouted the host.

"Oh, sorry, sir."

McManus looked at his watch and found it was later than he thought. He rose to his feet, abruptly, without finishing his lamb.

"I'm going for my rest, now," he said. "No doubt, I'll see you soon, O'Cassidy."

Marion and Vernon continued to eat. She was the first to break the silence.

"I hope my father didn't frighten you too much. He has the reputation of being a daunting man. He gets these melancholy fits."

"Why does he always bark?"

"I should have told you before. I didn't, because you were in such a state. It's nothing personal. He's all right with women, but he hates other men."

"Why?" asked Vernon.

"I don't really know. There are a lot of women who can't get on with other women. It's the same with my father. He despises members of his own sex."

"He's certainly a frightening man, but underneath his arresting manner, probably has a very kind heart," ventured Vernon, adding, "It's only natural for a father to be concerned about his daughter's security."

"Do you think so? You heard him threatening to take away my house and car, didn't you?"

"It was obvious it was only an empty threat," said Vernon, truthfully.

"Do you want to go to the Kevin Barry College?"

"I feel I should, particularly if your father's going to pay. Besides, I need some self respect. I've never done any proper work in my life."

Vernon attended the college. He found the work morbid and depressing, but stayed to the end of the course and gained a diploma.

There was one thing interfering with his ability to learn as fast as his colleagues. Now that his memory had returned, he was haunted by the events in the Hogg's Back Hotel, and the fear that his brothers would find him. These two things occupied his mind throughout his waking hours, and to help him forget, he was drinking as much as one and a half bottles of whisky a day.

Several years passed. Vernon had increased his alcohol consumption to two bottles of whisky a day. He looked older than his years. His face was drawn and permanently sweating, and his skin was coarse and yellow. He was then speaking with a natural Irish accent.

McManus, the hot-tempered funeral director had been dead for a year. His death occurred outside his offices on a hot day, when he was so short-staffed that he had to change the wheel of one of his hearses, himself. One of the few members of his staff on duty, a man called Kelly, was sauntering back to the offices after a liquid lunch with his girlfriend.

A wave of naked fear surged through Kelly when he saw his boss, kneeling in the gutter. He was swearing audibly. His sleeves were rolled up, and his hands and forearms were covered in oil.

"Sure, I could have done that for you, sir," murmured Kelly, breathing a heavy whiff of alcohol into his boss's face.

McManus looked up from his task, chewing the end of a fat cigar.

"You're too fockin' late!" he shouted. "You're

fired." Suddenly, his eyes widened and he clutched his throat with both hands. Within seconds, he was dead.

Marion had married Vernon and had taken the name, O'Cassidy, although the business remained in her father's name. They had an eight-year-old son, Caspar Patrick. Marion wished to carry on working, so she hired a sweet-natured, apple-cheeked Norland nanny who was English.

The child inherited his mother's looks and tough, resilient temperament, and lacked his father's effete, pathetic genes. He was a precocious boy, and was unaccustomed to mincing his words. He resented his father's drinking habits and neither loved nor respected him.

"Why are you always so drunk, Daddy?" he asked with irritating repetition several times a day.

"Mind your own business, boy," his father invariably replied. He never played with his son and hardly ever spoke to him, unless when answering his impertinent questions.

The drink prevented him from showing any interest in him. He was sufficiently industrious to occupy McManus's old office each day, under the guise of funeral director. His attendance was caused solely by his dwindling desire for self respect, and Marion hired an extra member of staff to handle his workload. Vernon sat at his desk and drank all day, covering his bottle of whisky with a brown paper bag.

One evening, after Caspar had gone to bed, Marion tackled him.

"Your drinking is having a bad effect on Caspar," she said, "and I don't care for it, either. In other words, I'm giving you an ultimatum. I'm calling our family doctor out tomorrow, with a view to putting you in hospital to dry out. If you refuse, I'm going to have to divorce you."

Vernon still loved her, and the idea of wandering through the streets of Dublin, with nowhere to sleep, was an anathema to him.

"All right. I'll do it," he said.

The family doctor's name was Dr Ryan. He was elderly, tired and disinterested, but agreed to admit Vernon to a hospital specializing in alcohol withdrawal.

"I'd like you to give him a full examination before you admit him," Marion stated.

Vernon was in the spare bedroom on the top floor of Marion's Queen Anne house. He had no interest in his predicament and need to withdraw from alcohol, although he was worried about his generalized feeling of seediness, and afraid that Marion would leave him.

Dr Ryan examined him but told him nothing of his findings. He went downstairs and found Marion in the drawing room.

"What's your opinion?" she demanded.

"I've told him nothing," he replied, "but you should know he's not a well man. The whites of his eyes are about as yellow as his skin. His tongue is blackened and furry. His breath is unspeakable and his liver is enlarged. I've taken some blood. I won't know whether his liver's been damaged, before I get the results. The Hospital of Our Blessed Virgin has a bed for him. I'm afraid there are no private rooms, so he'll be on an open ward."

"Serves him right! Is withdrawal very unpleasant?"

"No. We use Heminevrin these days. It's a painless drug which stops the craving. I'll let you know the results of the tests in a day or two."

The results showed that Vernon's liver was on the verge of becoming cirrhotic. He was in hospital for six weeks, and although the Heminevrin helped him, his withdrawal symptoms were horrific.

He was surrounded by twenty other patients with the same problem, which depressed him further, and he was unwilling to enter into a spirit of camaraderie with them. Also, the nurses were overworked and in short supply, which resulted in their being irritable, particularly towards patients with self-induced illnesses.

Each night, a nurse walked round the ward and

shone a torch on the patients, to make sure none of them were having choking fits. Vernon was woken by the nurse on duty. The sight of a torch being shone straight at his face, filled him with nausea and instinctive fear of his brothers.

"Do you mind, not shining that torch straight at me. It's terrifying!" he shouted.

"I'm just doing my night check. Those are my orders. There's no need to shout. You're waking everyone up."

Vernon felt the bile rise to his throat.

"Get me a basin. Hurry!" he commanded.

"What would you be wanting a basin for at this hour of night?" asked the nurse, thoughtlessly.

Vernon leant over the side of the bed and was sick on the floor.

"I've got liver damage, you stupid wanker!" he bellowed.

He was able to go home within six weeks. Marion was overjoyed when she saw him looking so much better, but Caspar, who had been unable to get to know him, was indifferent to his return. Dr Ryan had retired, and his practice was run by his junior partner, Dr O'Farrell, who took an interest in Vernon and visited the house once a week.

It was early February, 1995. Vernon swore to himself that he would have nothing to drink until

17th March, which was St Patrick's Day, when he planned to visit an IRA pub, called Biddy O'Rafferty's. He wanted to be swept off his feet by the bustle and excitement of revolutionary fanaticism. He crossed off each day of the calendar on his office wall, to cause the time to pass more quickly, and enable him to look forward to an evening of abandoned drunkenness.

He knew that he had been diagnosed as having a condition bordering on cirrhosis of the liver. Although the state of his liver obsessed him, the obsession was so painful that he made up his mind, if illogically, to drown himself with drink, and continue doing so from 17th March onwards.

O'Rafferty's was already crowded when Vernon went there at 7.00 in the evening. In a corner of the room, well away from the bar, a band played Irish rebel songs, and a man, whose body was draped in the Sinn Fein flag, sang loudly and passionately into a microphone, causing the building to vibrate.

Vernon was dressed in frayed black trousers, an off-white T-shirt and a black leather jacket. He edged his way through the dense crowd, and because of his troublesome abstinence from drink, he felt he was in paradise on reaching the bar. There were so many people in the pub that there was a shortage of glasses, and the drinks were served in plastic beakers.

Vernon smiled at the barman. His urge for a drink after so long, was so overpowering that he was almost prepared to kill for it.

"What will you have?" asked the barman. He was exhausted but felt happy because of the general feeling of *bonhomie* around him. He returned Vernon's smile.

"Two double whiskies," said Vernon. He backed into the crowd and drained both the plastic beakers, out of the barman's eyeshot. He went back to the bar.

"Two more double whiskies," he said, adding, defensively, "I've got my friends here with me. We've all come to celebrate."

On other occasions, the barman would have seen through the lie he had been told, and would have refused to sell any more alcohol to a customer whom he thought had had enough. He gave Vernon two more beakers.

Vernon went over to a vacant chair near an open door. He felt well and was no longer anxious about his dwindling health, or about the possibility of his brothers finding and killing him. The cold fresh air and breeze refreshed him. It was not long before he made repeated journeys to the bar, and by 10.00 o'clock, he had already consumed three quarters of a bottle of whisky.

The band broke into a robust rendering of a long, black-humoured song, composed by The Dubliners, about an IRA man being caught with bombing equipment in London. It was called *The Old Alarm Clock*, and its words held a morbid fascination for Vernon.

When first I came to London, in the year of '69,
The city, it was wonderful, and the girls, they were divine.
But the coppers got suspicious, and they soon gave me the knock.
I was charged with being the owner of an old alarum clock.

Next morning, down Great Marlborough Street, I caused no little stir.
The IRA were busy and the telephones did burr.
Said the Judge, "I'm going to charge you with the possession of this machine,
And I'm also going to charge you with the wearing of the Green."

"Now," says I to him, "Your Honour, if you'll give me half a chance,
I'll show you how this small machine can make the people dance.
It will tick away politely, 'till you get an awful shock,

*And it ticks away the gelig-in-ite and the old
             alarum clock."*

*The Judge said, "Look 'ee here, my man, and I'll
             tell you of my plan.
That you and I be countrymen, I could not give
             a damn.
And I am going to give you thirty years in
             Dartmoor dump,
And you can count that by the tickin' of your old
             alarum clock."*

*The lonely Dartmoor prison would put many in
             the jigs.
The cell, it isn't pretty, and it isn't very big,
But I'd long ago have left the place if I had
             only got
Ah, me couple of sticks of gelig-in-ite and me
             old alarum clock.*

At the other end of the pub, stood a stout, rough-looking, bearded man in a paint-stained denim suit. He was a tough, revolutionary psychopath who had volunteered to take part in an IRA cell, and his name was Dermot.

He was holding a vicious-looking, underfed Alsatian dog by its leather-studded collar, and at its feet, was a large, black, plastic bucket, once used as a lavatory, in a house which had only recently been equipped with plumbing facilities.

Dermot flung a wad of banknotes and coins into the foul-smelling bucket. He stroked the dog, which he had trained personally to pass the bucket round, to collect funds for the IRA, holding its handle between its teeth.

Dermot turned to his friend, a member of his cell.

"In a minute, you'll see how well I've trained Shamie. He's cleverer than a human. I'd say he was psychic. He can smell a Brit anywhere, and even knows if there's blood on his hands, shed with a motive, disconnected with the Cause."

"That's rubbish," said the cell member. "No dog has the power to find these things out. You've had a few too many."

"Why don't you watch? I can prove to you I'm right. There's a Brit I know of somewhere in this room. He's been pissing up at the bar for three hours."

"Oh? Who's he?"

"He's an undertaker from somewhere in Murphy Street. I don't' know his name, only his reputation. Everyone in Dublin knows about him. He was in the asylum, once. He's the man who emptied a box of golf balls over his psychiatrist's head."

Dermot released the dog's collar and patted it on

the back.

"Off you go, Shamie. Bring back lovely wads of money."

The multitude of customers in the pub, some overtly the worse for wear, patted and caressed the dog as it carried the bucket, from one person to another, leaving no-one out. Its lean, hungry look, made them afraid of refusing to give donations, for fear that it would go for their throats.

By the time it reached Vernon, dancing drunkenly in front of the band, it let the handle of the bucket fall from its mouth. The bucket was almost brimming with coins and banknotes, the latter amounting to two hundred pounds.

Vernon was puzzled. At first, his thieving instincts told him to pocket as many of the banknotes as he could, and rush off with them. The dog backed away from the bucket. Its whole body went rigid and it snarled at him as if wishing to eat him alive.

Other customers, who knew Dermot, and were familiar with the extraordinary powers of the dog, to suss out someone disconnected with Irish Republicanism, stared at Vernon with hostility.

Vernon sensed that there was something frightening and surreal about the dog. The extra strain he had put on his already damaged liver, caused a violent wave of nausea to surge through him. He knelt on the floor, and was copiously sick into the bucket, drowning most of the banknotes and making them invalid.

A few members of the crowd edged towards him with murder in their hearts. Vernon screamed, and rushed out of one of the open doors into the night.

He went to his office the next morning with a bottle of whisky, wrapped in a brown paper bag, in his briefcase. He locked himself in and stared wistfully at his mother's photograph on his empty desk. His gloom about his condition deepened, and to blot it out, he took a few swigs.

He grew restless, and walked via the unchanged, ostentatious front office into the street. His restlessness turned into severe agitation. He paced up and down, repeatedly covering the distance between O'Hara's offices and his own. He put the bottle to his lips once more.

"Hey! I'd be liking a word with you."

The voice was that of a man advancing towards him from the other side of the street. He had been walking with his head bowed. He failed to notice the man, and was unaware that he was addressing him.

"Hey! Are you deaf?"

"I'm sorry. I didn't know it was me you were speaking to. Is there something the matter?"

It was Dermot, the dog-trainer, who had come

to see him. His eyes were bloodshot and he was hung over. Despite his alcoholic haze, Vernon noticed that Dermot was unarmed, and knew that his anger was due to the incident at O'Rafferty's the previous night.

"I want your name!" shouted Dermot.

Vernon felt as if he were about to fall over. He turned his head and read the names of his offices and those of his rivals.

"I want your name!" repeated Dermot. "I could come back tomorrow!"

"Er, Paddy O'Hara," said Vernon.

"I'm glad you told me."

"Why?"

"Because this won't be the last time you'll hear from me. You've robbed us of two hundred pounds. We can't be using the banknotes, now. You were sick over the fockin' money!"

O'Hara was sitting in the passenger seat of his firm's only hearse. He was accompanied by his driver with whom he had an open, easy-going relationship. Two limousines, crammed with the relatives of the deceased, followed closely in O'Hara's wake.

"I've something to cheer you up, sir," said the driver.

"Let's have it," said O'Hara. He was in a jovial mood as so many former clients of McManus's were defecting to his firm.

"That man, who's taken over from McManus, is always drunk."

"Always drunk, you say?"

"Yes. He even drinks in the street. Only recently, when sitting in the passenger seat of one of his firm's hearses, he had a brown paper bag in his hand, which he was seen raising in the direction of his head."

O'Hara let out a guffaw and slapped his thigh.

"I want more stories! It's O'Cassidy you mean, isn't it?"

"Yes, sir."

The driver accounted for a myriad of occasions on which Vernon had been drunk, incapable and unable to hold his bile.

O'Hara rolled about in his seat, convinced that these were happy times indeed.

When he and his driver, and the drivers of the two limousines, returned from the funeral, his face froze and his heart almost stopped beating.

His offices, and everything they had contained, had been burnt out.

Marion returned home, at 5.30, and was irritated,

finding Vernon lying on his back in bed, out cold.

She prodded him in the chest.

"In one of your drunken stupors, again, I see. For God's sake, wake up!"

Vernon stirred himself with an effort and eased his weight onto his elbows.

"Have you heard the wonderful news?" she said.

"What wonderful news?"

"Someone's burnt O'Hara's offices out. That means we'll be getting all their trade. It's very odd, all the same. It's not as if their firm had had anything controversial or political about it."

"No," said Vernon, disinterestedly.

"Have you seen anyone suspicious, loitering in the street, recently?"

"No. I've been in my office all day."

"In your office, drinking all the time?"

"No. Not all the time. Only some of the time."

"You know when I told you I'd leave you if you didn't stop?"

"Yes."

"It wasn't true and it isn't now. I'll never leave you. Your drinking is an illness, not a crime."

"Part of the trouble is that I haven't told you the whole truth about my past," said Vernon, who was so ill that he no longer cared whether she left him or not.

"You told me of your paranoid fears about your brothers," she said.

"There's information I deliberately held from you, because I was afraid of losing you."

"Go ahead and tell me, then. Whatever it is, it won't interest me, not if it's something about the distant past."

"I told you once that my family tried to make me commit a murder. I said I refused and came to Ireland. I was lying."

"You were lying?"

"I did as I was told. I was ordered to kill a tycoon's wife's lover. I messed the whole thing up. I wasn't taking due care, and I shot the tycoon's wife."

"You mistook the tycoon's wife for her lover?"

"No. I didn't check that the gun was pointing at the right person."

"I suppose you were drunk," said Marion.

"A little. Then, because I was asked to shoot her lover, I shot him, too, at close range as he lay underneath her. That wasn't the only thing that went wrong. There was this tiresome brownhatter in the room next to me. He tried to kill himself because of unrequited love. He locked onto me and wouldn't leave me alone.

"I took him out for a walk in the woods and tried to kill him. Instead, I only knocked him out.

I buried him under some branches, thinking he was dead. I was dumbfounded when he came back to my room.

"I lured him to the room the other side of mine, where the man and woman I told you about, lay dead. I shot him, too, and left the gun in his hand, to make it look as if he'd committed suicide. All these things happened before I came to Ireland."

"Nothing about you has ever surprised me," said Marion, "but your story is so bizarre, that I suspect you're making it up."

"I wish I were," said Vernon, "but I'm not. It's not so much my brothers and my nagging worry that my liver is beyond repair. It's the horrible sight of those three bodies, the third one slumped over the other two. That's what haunts me during my waking hours, and the sight of all that blood.

"I took life from a young man with his entire future ahead of him, and on top of that, I took life from a man and woman who would have probably married, their hearts awash with happiness. Now that I've told you this sickening and revolting story, do you still want me to stay?"

"You were wise not to tell me when we first met," said Marion. "I would have been wary of sharing my bed with a serial killer. You've told me so long after the event. The whole thing doesn't seem real enough to merit my doing something so dramatic as asking you to leave me. It is disgusting and distressing, but somehow, it belongs to another world.

"The fact that you were bullied into it by your family, whom it would have been difficult for you to disobey, doesn't make it seem quite so bad. Your confession confirms what has always been my view. You are a weak, stupid, frail, cowardly drunk. All these characteristics make you vulnerable, and draw out my maternal instinct which makes me love you more."

Vernon thought that his confession would cleanse his conscience and enable him to stop drinking. He had hoped to find solace in halving his troubles by sharing them, but the sound of his voice releasing them in the air, actually worsened them. He still withheld the information about his murder of O'Cassidy. Instead of feeling relieved, and closer to his wife, he felt undignified and berated himself for having told her.

He drank even more heavily for the next few months, increasing his intake to two and a half bottles of whisky a day. His skin became even yellower than it had been before his stay in hospital. His face was damp with sweat and his body shook as if he had Parkinson's Disease. Even then, he refused to see the retired Dr Ryan's junior partner, Dr O'Farrell, through terror of being told what he had done to his liver.

Vernon was intolerant of hot weather which reminded him of the four murders he had committed. August, 1995 was even more sweltering than any period during the traumatic, hot summer of 1963. He spent all his time lying on his back with a fan on, two feet away from him, blowing straight at his face. Although nauseated and frail, he was not too weak to lean out of bed to pick up his bottle of whisky.

Marion came home at 5.30, looking worried and agitated. She was carrying an English newspaper under her arm. A few swigs of whisky had given Vernon temporary strength. He sat up.

"Hullo, Marion."

"I'm afraid I have very sad news for you," she said, without looking him in the eye.

"Yes?"

"When we first met, you told me your real name was Eddy Vernon, didn't you?"

"That's right."

"You also said you had two brothers."

"Yes."

"Is Olive Vernon your mother's name?"

"Yes, it is. Has something happened to her?"

Marion sat down on the bed and took his hand.

"According to an article I read in this paper,

I'm afraid your mother's just died."

"She's died? What did she die of?"

"She had cancer. Here, have a look at the article."

Vernon's shaking hands held the paper. The article, headed "East End Gangster Mother Bites Dust," read, "Olive Vernon, notorious but well-liked head of a London East End gangster family, died yesterday in the London Hospital, Whitechapel, following a six month fight against cancer. She leaves two sons, Kelvin and Alan, who have so far avoided being caught red-handed. Olive had a third son, Eddy who was found dead in an underground carpark in West Smithfield in 1963. He had committed suicide. Olive is expected to have a spectacular Mafia-style funeral at All Souls Church in Bethnal Green on 1 September, 1995."

Vernon expected Marion to demand an explanation for his "suicide", but she appeared to know what had happened. She said,

"This is one thing you didn't tell me. You met an Irishman called O'Cassidy somewhere in London in 1963. You lured him to an underground carpark. You held him up at gun point, and told him to exchange his clothes and papers for yours, didn't you?"

"Yes," muttered Vernon.

"How did you kill him?"

"I slit his throat with a razor blade to make his death look like suicide, and left the blade on the concrete," he said, adding defensively, "I made a point of wearing gloves to avoid leaving my prints on the blade. That's the kind of man I am. If you had any sense, you'd throw me out. I don't care if you do. I'll soon be dead, anyway."

"No," she said. "Whatever you did, I can't do that. You're my husband. You've never done me any harm, so it's my duty to protect you, particularly as you're ill. However, I must insist on one thing. You're to go to see Dr O'Farrell and get your liver function tests done."

"I'm afraid to. I don't want to be told it's too late."

"If you refuse to go, I'll have to turn you in. I'll make an appointment for us both to see him tomorrow."

Vernon turned his head to the wall and sunk into a stupor.

"Ah, Mr and Mrs O'Cassidy, come in and sit down," said Dr O'Farrell in a friendly, welcoming tone. He was strong in build, fortyish and his rust-coloured hair was parted in the centre.

O'Farrell leant over his desk and stared aghast at Vernon, fearing he would soon be losing his custom.

"Mr O'Cassidy. I won't waste time. I'll come straight to the point. Apparently, you were admitted to hospital sometime this year, under my retired colleague, Dr Ryan. Your wife rang me early this morning and told me you have been drinking two and a half bottles of whisky a day for some time. It's no good your denying it. I can tell, just by looking at you, that you've been beating your poor, wretched liver black and blue."

"I'm not attempting to deny it," said Vernon.

"It may not be too late, though. I'll run a battery of tests which will mean my having to take blood. There are three enzymes governing liver function. For your interest, they are gamma GT, alanine transferase and aspartate transaminase. In your case, these are obviously out of alignment."

O'Farrell asked Vernon to lie down on a couch behind a screen, and gave him a painful blood test with a thick-needled hypodermic. Once he had put the blood into a labelled tube, he ran his hand gently over the right hand side of Vernon's stomach.

"Just as I thought," he said. "If you'll pardon my grim humour, your liver is what we call a brutally battered wife. It's swollen up like a Rugby ball."

"Do you think it's cirrhosis, doctor?"

O'Farrell left the covered area and walked over to Marion who was crying.

"I don't wish to commit myself at this stage. I'll know when I get the results of the tests."

"When will that be?" asked Vernon urgently.

"They should come through in about a week. Things move very slowly here, particularly in August, when a lot of the lab technicians are on holiday. I'll take your telephone number if I may."

"We have a mobile 'phone," said Marion. "My husband likes to carry it around with him. The number's 0370422309."

"Good. I've written that down. In the meantime, Mr O'Cassidy, I'd prefer it if you didn't drink."

"I'll have to drink for the next few days. I've got to go to London to attend my mother's funeral."

"Oh, I'm so sorry, sir."

"Yes. Her death has come as an awful shock. Also, I'm worried sick about my health, and the stress is worse than the illness itself. Once my mother's funeral is behind me, I'll go into hospital like I did before. I'll keep the mobile 'phone on all the time, until I get your call."

"I'm glad to hear that, Mr O'Cassidy."

"Do you think I stand a chance?"

"I won't know until I see the results. There's no point in despairing before we know exactly what you've done to yourself."

He ushered Vernon and Marion out. Once he had the room to himself, he picked up his gold Parker pen and made a terse entry in Vernon's file. He wrote "P.B.B.B." which in medical jargon means, Pine Box By Bed.

Vernon staggered to his solicitor's office the following day, and made out a Will, which he was told he could collect in two days' time.

He, Marion, Caspar and the nanny, were due to travel by train to London the day before Olive Vernon's funeral. Marion had arranged accommodation in a nondescript hotel in the Cromwell Road, and a London branch of the McManus firm was told to provide two limousines to take them to the East End.

Marion, Caspar and the nanny were sitting in the kitchen, having breakfast, before they were due to leave Dublin. Vernon's trembling hands were nailing his Will to the wall. In his drunken state, he thought it would be more secure in his house than in his solicitor's office.

Caspar was fascinated by his strange father's behaviour.

"What's Daddy doing, Mummy?"

"He's nailing his Will to the wall," Marion replied in a flat, blunted, despairing tone.

"Why?"

"Because that must be where he wishes to put it," was all she could think of answering.

Vernon and Marion occupied the first of the two limousines bound for Olive's funeral on the warm, damp September morning. Caspar and the nanny, who had a comforting, calming and stabling effect on him, travelled behind them.

"Nanny?" said Caspar.

"Speaking, my boy," she said, smiling.

"Is Daddy ill?"

"Why, no. Not ill. At least, not exactly, anyway."

"Why does he lie down all day?"

"Perhaps, he feels tired."

"Is it true that he drinks whisky from the time he gets up to the time he goes to sleep?"

"Now, now, you mustn't be impertinent about your father's personal habits."

"But he always looks so ill. Is he?"

"Why, I would have to be a doctor to answer that, wouldn't I, my boy?"

There was a pause broken by Caspar.

"Nanny?"

"Yes."

"May I tell you a joke?"

"Of course, you can. We need a bit of comic relief to brighten up a sad occasion."

"I'm afraid it's rude."

"If it's rude, I don't want to hear it, do I, dear?"

The two limousines arrived inappropriately early at the church in Bethnal Green, just before 12.30. Vernon went straight into the church, and left Marion alone. The nanny had no wish to sit in a claustrophobic car with her charge, until the funeral at 2.00 o'clock. She went for a walk round the cemetery with him, despite the rain.

The cemetery was deserted, and the nanny was particularly surprised by the sight of a ragged, weather-beaten woman, a gypsy, walking purposefully towards her and Caspar. The closer she got to them, the more apparent it became that she had something urgent to say.

"Can I take a minute of your time?" The woman had a strange, West Country accent.

"What do you want?" asked the nanny suspiciously.

"You are both in great danger."

"What of? You've never met us before."

"I don't need to have met you before. You work for the man who went into that church five minutes ago. I didn't see inside the church, but I know he is sitting in the second pew closest to the aisle."

"How on earth do you know that?" asked the nanny, astounded.

"I know these things. I don't have to be told."

"What are you trying to tell me?"

"It's not you I'm concerned with," said the gypsy. "It's the man you serve."

"What about him?"

"I can tell you one thing, and one thing only."

"Yes?"

"If you don't make him leave the church straight away, my friend, he'll be dead before the day is out. This is the last warning I'll give you."

"You silly woman, what stuff and nonsense you do talk!" replied the nanny.